GUNS OF THE BRASADA

Ballard and McCall are in Texas, working for Henry Conway, an old friend, on the Lazy-C ranch. But trouble is brewing: Yancey Merrick, owner of the big Diamond-M, keeps pushing to expand his empire. Then Henry's son Harry is run down through the brasada thicket before being shot in the back and killed. Determined to find the guilty party, Ballard and McCall suddenly find themselves deep in a developing range war . . .

NEIL HUNTER

GUNS OF THE BRASADA

Complete and Unabridged

LINFORD
Leicester

First published in Great Britain in 2015

First Linford Edition
published 2017

A catalogue record for this book is available
from the British Library.

ISBN 978–1–4448–3115–3

Published by
F. A. Thorpe (Publishing)
Anstey, Leicestershire

Set by Words & Graphics Ltd.
Anstey, Leicestershire
Printed and bound in Great Britain by
T. J. International Ltd., Padstow, Cornwall

This book is printed on acid-free paper

1

Chet Ballard found Harry Conway deep in the brasada. He lay in a forlorn bundle, his unprotected body carrying two 44–40 rifle slugs in his back. He was also badly cut and slashed from being chased through the unforgiving brush country, his flesh torn and scarred and his clothing blood-soaked. The wild thicket was home to numerous and varied species of plant life, each equipped with its own armament of thorns and barbs. Prickly-pear, cat's-claw, Spanish dagger, black chaparral, twisted acacia and mesquite. The tracks Ballard had been following for the past couple of miles testified to what had happened.

Dismounting, Ballard crouched over the body and knew straight off that this had been murder plain and simple, but with an added twist that made it downright cruel. Conway was only clad in his range clothes. Thick shirt and Levis. When Ballard had seen the younger man the previous day he had been wearing the added gear any man working the brasada would protect himself with. Thick leather leggings and long leather gloves. A sturdy coat as well. All necessary additions there for protection from the vicious barbs that grew in abundance. As young as he had been Conway was a native born Texan, familiar with the brasada. He had been working the country for years and knew the dangers. There was no way he would have ventured into the thicket without protection.

Ballard saw the protective clothing scattered across the ground where Conway had been forced to abandon it.

Examining the blood-stained body Ballard understood what had happened. Conway had been compelled to run for his life. Set afoot and pursued by a man who knew exactly what they were doing. A deadly chase that had ended when someone had put two slugs in Conway's back and left him to be found. There had been a sadistic pleasure taken by the killer. A need to make Harry Conway suffer before his life had been ended by the bullets in his back. That took a particularly twisted mind.

Sitting on his heels Ballard pushed his hat back, eyes scanning the immediate area, looking for something. Anything that might give him a clue as to who had done this. There were no close hoof prints. No surprise there. The killer would have been able to shoot from a distance. Ballard rose and began to pace back the way Conway had come. His boot prints were still visible and there were spots of dried blood from the cuts inflicted by the sharp thorns of the undergrowth. Pushing upright Ballard followed the ragged line of boot prints. Conway had been moving from side to side, trying to avoid the thickets. After a few hundred yards Ballard saw the churned-up patch of earth where a horse had stood, hoofs restless as its rider hauled up on the reins. Most likely where the man had halted to dismount and track Conway before making his killing shots.

Sunlight glinted to one side. Ballard bent and picked up two shiny brass shell casings. Still dry and unmarked. They couldn't have been there more than a few hours. He examined them. They were 44–40 caliber, most likely from a rifle.

And it had taken two of them to end Conway's life.

Ballard looked around, knowing as he did that whoever had fired those shots would be long gone. No back shooter would stay around once the deed had been done.

He found boot prints where the shooter had stood. Something about them made Ballard crouch to examine them closer. They were small and narrow, the toes coming almost to a point. Ballard held the image in his mind as he stood and went to where

Harry Conway lay.

He bent over Conway and took hold, lifting the younger man in his arms as if he had been a child. Conway had been full grown, but the six-foot-six Texan held him easily as he turned around and carried him back to where his horse stood. It was no effort for Ballard to lay the limp body across his saddle. It was as he settled the dead man Ballard noticed that Conway's sixgun was not in its holster.

Disarmed and forced to run for his life.

As Ballard gently tied Conway down and laid his blanket over him, he felt his slow-burning anger starting to show itself. He had to take a step back and let the feeling subside.

Ballard took the reins and led his horse and its burden back out of the thicket. Back a ways his partner Jess McCall was carrying out a search of his own. They had both been looking for Conway since his loose horse had wandered back into the line camp. It took Ballard a half hour before he picked up the sound of a rider. He saw the man and waved his hat.

Jess McCall reined in, his expression changing when he saw the blanketed body.

'Not Harry,' he said.

Ballard nodded. 'Somebody set him afoot. Made him shuck his protective outfit and forced him to run for his life through the thicket . . . before they put a pair of slugs in his back.'

The big Texan let go a sigh as he studied the covered form. The expression mirrored his thoughts. Out and out murder, which was how this shaped up, would take the current situation over the line from simple harassment to nothing less than a range war. As disappointed as he was McCall realized he wasn't all that surprised. It was the way things had been shaping up over the last couple of months.

McCall and his partner, Ballard, had been taking pay from Henry Conway for the last six months. The spread's owner had known Ballard for years, and Ballard had seen Harry Conway grow from a young boy into a hard-working man and they had been friends. Now Ballard was going to see Harry buried.

Since signing on with the brand, Ballard and McCall had been working the Lazy-C range alongside the rest of the crew in and around the brasada country. It was tough country, the work hard, but Conway's crew was experienced and they were fiercely loyal to their employer. As Texicans themselves, Ballard and McCall had fitted in well. Since joining forces following their first meeting they had partnered up permanently, riding together and getting into and out of scrapes, taking jobs when they became necessary, and now they were drawing pay and working cattle and that had been something they took to easily.

Things had started to change once Yancey Merrick and his Diamond-M outfit moved into the area. It had been obvious from the start that Merrick had his eyes set on dominating the area. He had a big crew on his payroll. To a man they were hard, swaggering individuals, prone to pushing their way around and from the day Merrick brought his own herd in and established his spread trouble reared its head. Merrick made it known he intended to become the biggest outfit in the area. He had the influence and the backing of money to do it. It soon became obvious he intended to dominate the local range.

The town of Beecher's Crossing, established for years, provided all the services the surrounding spreads needed. It was a typical cattle country town. Nothing grand. Everything the spreads needed and some. Like any town built on the cattle business Beecher's Crossing had its share of trouble. Mainly from the ranch crews letting off steam when they had free time. There was nothing too serious for the town marshal, Ray Bellingham, to handle. Rowdy drunks. The occasional gunplay. Sometimes things got a little out of hand but the flare-ups fizzled out as quickly as they blew up.

Until Merrick's crew started to throw their weight around. Things got ugly a time or two. The Diamond-M began to push their way in with a way the town wasn't used to. If anything became too serious Merrick himself would come to town and smooth things over with his persuasive tongue and his ready cash. He was not slow in reminding the town merchants that since the Diamond-M had shown up there was a great deal more money being spent in Beecher's Crossing. Merrick had a sly way and he hit the town businessmen where they appreciated it — in their wallets. If any damage was done Merrick paid for it without a fuss. The man was no fool. He knew profit covered many sins and he used that to smooth over ruffled feathers.

Away from town there were signs the Diamond-M had eyes on other things. Like prime grazing land. Water. At first the incidents were small and isolated, but the signs were there. Cattle pushed off their usual ranges. Chased into the thickets. The odd fence cut and trampled down. And then a series of late night disturbances. Stored feed contaminated. A barn burned down. Stable doors opened and horses set free. The incidents created a climate of unease in the community. No one had solid proof the Diamond-M was behind the problems.

No one had proof — but folk just knew.

The atmosphere grew and flared into open hostility in town. The weekend fun started to turn ugly. And the Diamond-M men always seemed to be involved. Bar fights became a regular occurrence. In most instances it was a single cowhand picked on and goaded into a fight that quickly turned brutal with two or three Diamond-M hands dishing out beatings. Broken bones and bloody faces became the staple for the town doctor. Cracked ribs and the odd broken arm. It was getting out of hand.

For Henry Conway, owner of the Lazy-C, the increasing disturbances became personal. His spread had the best stretch of rangeland in the area. Good grazing and a natural water supply. The Lazy-C covered a big section of land, lying in a vast natural bowl that was bounded by gentle hills. On the southern curve of his range a natural barrier was created by the brasada itself. The sprawling thicket offered a protective stretch of terrain that separated the Lazy-C from its immediate neighbors.

Henry Conway ran an honest outfit and there was no man in the area who could say different. Conway was always on the front line when help was needed. His standing in Beecher's Crossing was as high as any man and he treated everyone as a friend. There were a number of people in town who owed Henry Conway for his help when they were down on their luck. That wasn't to say Conway was less a businessman. He had a solid head on his broad shoulders. He knew cattle and he knew how to operate his outfit.

He had come to the brasada country as a younger man with a dream of building his cattle empire, a few dollars in his pockets, and a burning ambition to become the best he could. Over fifteen years he had done that. Taking up his piece of range and staking it out. From nothing Conway had forged the Lazy-C out of the empty land. He had built his sprawling house, extending it as time went by. Building his stables and outhouses. The bunkhouse for his growing crew. He brought in his first small herds and bred good, sound Texas beef. Made drives and sold to the eager cattle companies. He took up contracts to supply the Chicago stockyards.

When Conway came to the area he had a young wife, a son and daughter. The business he created and fought Indians and outlaws to keep was for them. As the boy, Harry, grew into adulthood he became part of the Lazy-C crew. He worked alongside the rest of the cowhands, learning the business and becoming as proficient as any of the experienced riders. He was offered no favors and never asked for them. He was one of the Lazy-C crew.

Now he was being carried home over the back of his horse. Led by the silent Ballard and McCall who were secretly dreading the moment they had to tell Henry Conway his son was dead.

They had only just cleared the thicket when Henry Conway and a number of Lazy-C hands appeared, riding in their direction.

'*Oh, hell,*' McCall said quietly.

He glanced across at his partner and saw Ballard had taken off his hat, holding it across his lap. Right at that moment McCall wished he was anywhere but here. He watched the bunch of riders moving in close. Took off his own weather-beaten Stetson.

Henry Conway must have immediately recognized his son's favorite paint pony. He sat upright and spurred his own mount forward, bringing it to a tight-reined halt in front of Ballard. Conway leaned forward in his saddle, clutching the horn with his big, gloved hands, and he knew without a spoken word who lay under the blanket. The big shoulders stiffened and when Conway raised his head to look directly at Ballard the grief was there in his eyes, tears already welling up. He took a shuddering breath, struggling to contain himself as he relived in a fleeting moment all the years that had just been wiped away.

'What happened, Chet?'

'No way to say it easy, Henry.'

'Then don't, son, just give me the words.'

'Somebody caught him by the thicket. Made him take off his leathers and ran him through the brasada before they backshot him.'

Someone behind Conway muttered in anger. A second voice followed suit.

'Easy, boys,' Conway said. He dismounted and crossed to the blanket covered form. 'I need to see.'

Conway loosened the tie rope and drew the blanket free, exposing the body. He stared at the bloody corpse, then drew in a ragged breath, leaning against the horse for support.

'*Sweet Jesus*,' he said in a voice so low only Ballard and McCall heard. 'Look what they did to my boy.'

Jess McCall stepped from his saddle, his tall figure moving to stand behind Conway. He placed his big, work-scarred hands on his employer's shoulders.

'Let us bring him home, Henry. You'll want to go on ahead and speak to the missus.'

At the mention of his wife Conway let go a soft moan.

'God, how do I tell her? This will destroy her.'

'Henry, you'll be there for her. Helen is strong,' McCall said. 'Leave us to bring your boy home while you tell her what happened.'

One of the Lazy-C hands edged his horse forward. His name was Laney Chancery. A tall and spare man in his mid-forties. Chancery had been with Conway for many years. He was the ranch foreman. His narrow face, with its dark and soulful eyes, showed the hard life he had endured as a working hand. He had a pale, puckered scar running across his left cheek, the reward for a lax moment when dealing with a recalcitrant steer many years back. He wore a thick, drooping mustache that was his pride and joy.

'We'll ride to the house, Henry,' he said gently. He normally had a hushed voice and at that moment it was exactly the right tone needed. 'Boys'll bring Harry to home. You come on now. Let's get her done.'

He led Conway to his horse. Got him back in the saddle and led out with a nod in Ballard and McCall's direction.

2

They buried Harry Conway two days later, near the stand of cottonwoods east of the big house where the shade lay a gentle hand across the ground. Neighbors from outlying ranches came to join with the entire Lazy-C crew and the Rev Behan came from Beecher's Crossing along with a number of the town dignitaries. The town's lawman, Ray Bellingham, came. It was a well attended funeral and Rev Behan spoke words over the grave.

After the service there was a gathering around the long trestle tables that had been set up and covered with Helen Conway's best linen cloths. With help from her daughter, Christine, and neighbor women she provided a good spread and there was no shortage of food and drink.

Helen Conway was a beautiful

woman in her early forties. The long years working beside her husband and building the Lazy-C and bringing up her two children had been hard. Despite this she had kept her looks. Today she held her own but there was no hiding the fact she was grieving for the son just lost. As she moved around the tables, speaking to neighbors, McCall didn't fail to notice the lost look in her eyes.

Like all the other men McCall wore a dark suit and white shirt, a thin string tie and his boots polished to a high sheen. He eased through the crowd until he was able to stand beside Helen, his tall figure dwarfing her.

'I get you anything, ma'am?' he asked.

'That's kind of you, Jess, but I believe I'm fine at the moment.'

Christine Conway joined them. In her early twenties, Chris, as she was always known, had her mother's looks combined with a strong personality and a brain to match. Close to her brother she had handled his death well, and even now she managed to stay in control of her emotions. Yet McCall knew she was hurting inside.

'Mom, why don't you take a minute. Everyone can help themselves now.' She smiled at McCall. 'Thanks for all your help, Jess.'

'No trouble.'

A subdued murmur came from the guests. McCall glanced over Helen's shoulder and saw three riders drawing rein on the approach to the house. He didn't need a second look to identify them.

'Damn,' McCall muttered

In the lead, astride the big black stallion he always rode was Yancey Merrick, owner of the Diamond-M. Even at a distance he cut an impressive figure. Dressed as always he wore a black suit obviously tailored to fit. His wide-brimmed Stetson, now laid across his lap, was also black, and the hand-tooled boots showing beneath the cuffs of his pants were custom-made. In

19

his forties, Merrick was a handsome man who carried himself well.

He turned and said something to the pair of riders with him and they followed a few yards behind their employer as Merrick spurred the big black towards the funeral gathering.

McCall knew one of the riders who had come with Merrick.

Rafe Kershaw. Lean and mean-faced, a heavy Colt hanging from his waist, the holster tied down. He was a gunhand, with a mean reputation. A man who hired himself out and wasn't too fussed how he earned his pay. If there was anyone behind the trouble brewing from the Diamond-M, Kershaw would be involved somewhere along the line.

McCall didn't know the second man, but he recognized the signs. Though he was dressed in range clothes, the rider wore a pair of matching revolvers, in well-cared-for holsters. He stared directly at McCall, his expression intended to intimidate the Texan.

As Merrick came closer Henry Conway eased his way through the gathered mourners and planted himself in front of the rider.

McCall felt Helen Conway's hand on his arm.

'Won't be any trouble,' the big Texan said, and crossed the yard to stand a few feet to one side of Henry Conway. He didn't speak. Simply made his presence felt. His coat was open, showing he wore no gun, but his six foot plus size was suggestion enough.

Merrick reined in some feet away from Conway. For a few seconds the two men faced each other in silence.

'Came to offer my condolences,' Merrick said. 'Seemed the right thing to do.'

'Now that's done you can leave,' Conway said. 'I'll give you one thing, Merrick. You got gall.'

If the brusque words offended Merrick he didn't show it. He inclined his head as if he was considering Conway's request.

'You lost your son,' he said finally. 'That should be an end to matters, except I believe you hold some kind of grievance.'

Conway sucked in his breath. Held his shoulders back.

'That the speech you give everyone the Diamond-M has trampled on?'

'Henry, I might take exception to what you're suggesting if I was a man who harbored a slight.'

'Let me tell you, here and now, Merrick. You ain't gettin' your hands on the Lazy-C. I staked my claim here a long time ago. Fit the weather. The Comanch'. Every creature on four and two legs and some that crawl on their bellies. And now you walk in and try to lay claim to the whole damn range. Now I can't prove it but I got my suspicions who's behind my son's murder. And I'm lookin' you straight in the eye, Merrick, so you take heed.'

Merrick leaned on his saddle-horn, gloved fingers gripping tight enough to make the leather creak.

'Harsh words, Mister Conway. But that's all they are and words don't mean a damn thing. I'll tell now. I'm here to stay and I got big plans for the area. One way or t'other the Diamond-M is going to get bigger. Just think on.'

McCall made an impatient movement of his head and shoulders, attracting Merrick's attention.

'Something bothering you?'

'Could say that. See I'm partial to the view from here. Only right now you and your boys are kind of blocking it. Be grateful if you could clear the way as you leave.'

Merrick stared at the big man, seeing the hard intention behind McCall's amiable expression.

'You . . .'

'Mister McCall to you. And tell that skinny little pissant, Kershaw, to keep his hand away from his gun there. He moves it any closer I'll spit in his eye. And I don't miss with that either.'

'I know you,' Kershaw said. 'Got yourself some kind of tough rep.'

'Funny that,' McCall said, 'I hardly heard anything about you and what I did wasn't worth the effort of listening.'

Kershaw's thin face colored and he gripped the Colt on his hip.

'What did I hear you say?'

'Deaf as well?' McCall said. 'No. You heard well enough.'

'You take out that gun, Kershaw, I'll put you behind bars.'

Kershaw's head turned and he stared at the speaker and found himself facing Ray Bellingham. The lawman, a solid man who took no nonsense from any man, wasn't wearing his gun, but the burnished badge pinned to his shirt displayed his authority. He ran the law in Beecher's Crossing and the surrounding territory with a firm hand. A well-respected man and not one to ever back down.

'*That son of a . . .*'

'You will tell that man of yours to curb his tongue, Yancey Merrick,' Helen Conway said. 'Bad enough you intrude on my son's funeral. I'll not tolerate your man's foul mouth.'

'The hell with this . . . ' Kershaw said. 'Time we . . . '

Merrick held up his hand. 'The lady is right, Rafe. Let it go. There'll be another time.' He touched the brim of his hat. 'My apologies, ma'am. Just remember this is hard country. For women as well as men.'

He swung his horse around and kicked it into motion. Kershaw, after a few seconds, followed. The third rider held his ground, studying the gathering as if he was remembering every face, nodding gently to himself. His dressed-down appearance went against the fancy double gun-rig he wore. He was lean-faced, tall even in the saddle.

'Something else you want?' Bellingham asked.

The man gave a hint of a smile. He switched his gaze to Ballard.

'Big hombre,' he said, as if he was remembering something.

Ballard returned the stare. 'Big enough, feller.'

25

'Now I heard of you,' he said. 'Seems there was a Ballard who made a name for himself down Waco way couple years back. He wore a badge then.'

'Waco? I've been there. Couple of years back.'

'Likely you knew Jeb Brookner.'

'Brookner? I knew him. Only for a short time. Got cut short when he tried to brace me.'

The man allowed a brief, angry flicker to show in his eyes.

'I heard what happened to Jeb.'

'Now you're going to tell me he was a friend.'

'A real good friend.'

'Hope you're not about to tell me he was kin.'

'Might as well have been. We ran together a long while.'

'In future I'd choose better,' Ballard said.

'Now I remember. That lawdog from Waco was the spittin' image of you. Even the name fits. Big feller. Walked tall and talked kind of easy.'

'I'm not wearing a badge now.'

'That don't bother me one way or t'other.'

'It should,' Bellingham said. 'I am wearing a badge, so stay peaceful, mister.'

'Don't imagine this is done. I'll see you soon, Ballard,' the man said. 'Your time's coming.'

The rider turned his horse and left.

Ballard stood his ground, big fists opening and closing as he absorbed what he had seen just as the rider moved away. His booted feet in the stirrups. Small feet. The custom-made boots narrow and coming to points. Just like the prints he'd seen out where Harry Conway had been killed.

There was a prolonged pause before McCall, who had been quietly watching the proceedings, edged up to his partner.

'You been stirring the pot again, I see.'

'Me?' Ballard said. 'I just like to figure out the opposition.'

'Take it easy with Ash Boynton,' Bellingham said, joining them.

'He that two-gun joker?' McCall said.

'Boynton might not dress up fancy,' Bellingham said, 'but don't allow it to fool you. He's smart and no slouch with those guns.'

'He wanted anywhere?' McCall asked.

Bellingham shook his head. 'That's the thing. He's never been involved in anything the law can pin on him. He has the confidence to let the other man draw first. Calls their bluff and then puts them down. Walks away every time. I also heard tell a few dead men were found with bullet holes in their backs while Boynton was around. Story goes he hires out to do the dirty work others don't have the stomach for. But no proof other than saloon talk.'

McCall caught the gleam in Ballard's eyes. He knew how his partner's mind worked and Ballard already had Boynton figured.

'So what did happen in Waco?' McCall asked.

'Brookner was a local yahoo who liked to push the line. Had a notion he was building himself a reputation. Saw himself as a fast gun. After I took down a couple of fellers who tried to rob the town bank, Brookner started in. Said he could take me. Wouldn't let it lie. Kept pushing until he got himself so worked up he forced a fight. I tried to walk away. He wouldn't. Put a shot in my side. So I turned around and shot back before he got off his second. Made mine count.'

'This Boynton wants a reckoning,' McCall said. 'Chet, you'll need to watch for him. Something tells me he's not about to forget.'

'Right now we've got other things to worry about,' Ballard said.

'Ray, Chet is right,' McCall said. 'Merrick is bound and determined to keep matters on the boil.'

'I know that,' Bellingham said. 'And

he's got his eye on the Lazy-C. That's no secret.'

And he has Ash Boynton on his payroll, Ballard thought.

Henry Conway spoke up. 'Murdering my son is just his way of getting through to me. He wants to scare me off. Well, he's in for a surprise if he expects me to step aside.'

'Henry, being able to arrest him would give me the greatest pleasure,' the lawman said. 'Right now there's nothing we can use against him. The man is ruthless. He's also smart.'

'Believe me, Ray, I understand,' Conway said.

He turned away. Suddenly he looked an old man. His shoulders slumped as Helen walked him towards the house.

Laney Chancery watched them go and the hurt on the cowboy's face said it all.

'I seen that man walk through all kinds of hell,' he said. 'First time I seen him helpless.'

He turned about and followed the Conways.

'I'll be keeping an eye on Merrick,' Bellingham said. 'Somewhere along the line he's going to make a mistake.'

'How many more folk got to be hurt before he does?' Ballard said.

Bellingham had no answer to that. There wasn't much he could do without real proof that Merrick was acting outside the law. Right now that was less than smoke in the wind.

After another hour the wake began to break up. After saying their goodbyes neighbors began to drift away. By late afternoon the ranch yard was deserted save for the crew and a couple of women helping to clear the tables.

'This is where it's going to hit them hard,' Ballard said. 'Long as they were busy it doesn't seem all that real.'

McCall loosened his tie and collar stud. Even he was having difficulty finding the right words. He stood watching the women moving around the tables.

'Chet, this just ain't right,' he said. 'That boy was out and out murdered. Left to die in the thicket and we're letting it go.'

Ballard had no argument with that. He felt the injustice as much as his partner.

'Who said anything about letting it go?'

McCall nodded. 'Glad to hear that. So you got a notion to find out who?'

'Damn right I do.'

'Let's do it,' McCall said.

'Let's take a ride come morning,' Ballard said.

And that's exactly what they did.

3

They rode out early, before the crew was up and about. It was promising to be another hot day, for which Ballard was grateful. There hadn't been any rain in the area since the shooting, so it was entirely possible tracks left behind might still be visible. Even McCall agreed it was a slight chance. They had to start somewhere and they both had a growing need to find out the reasons for Harry Conway's death.

Ballard had recognized the signs and he knew better than to even think about raising any objections. Not that he had any. Harry, despite being the boss's son, had been a good man to work with. If the truth were told Ballard saw his death as a tragedy. For all concerned.

It took them a couple of hours to reach the site of the killing. They had pulled on the gear needed to protect them from the brasada. Ballard led the way to the first set of tracks that had guided him to Harry Conway's body. He and McCall dismounted and tethered their horses, took their rifles, and stood looking around.

There were signs that showed a couple of horses had been present. They cast around, studying the fading hoof prints.

'That's where Harry rode in,' McCall said. 'He would have come from that direction. Searching for strays.'

'Other set comes in from the east.' Ballard hunkered down examining the hoof prints, then the marks left by riding boots. 'Both dismounted. Done some moving around until one set of boot prints head into the thicket.'

'Harry,' McCall said. 'Other man would have had his gun on him. Made him run for his life after he made him skin off his leathers. Harry had no choice. If he wanted to stay alive he had to risk the thicket. When I found him I picked him up and headed out.'

'So no one from the Lazy-C has been out here since?'

Ballard shook his head. 'Too much to be done. Staying to home. Getting Harry ready for his burying. Why?'

'So this is how you found it?'

'Guess so.'

McCall eyed his partner, sensing Ballard had something on his mind.

'You got anything you need to tell me?' he asked.

Ballard pointed out the set of boot prints he'd seen before. Even though they had faded the distinct formation was still visible.

'The shooter,' he said. 'Found the shell casings right next to them.'

'Small prints. Narrow. Not a woman?'

'A man's.'

'You sound sure.'

'I am.'

'Chet, I suspicion you might know who owns them.'

Ballard simply nodded. 'Keep that in mind.'

'We got a chance to pick up those tracks leading away. Maybe follow 'em back to where they came from before they get worn away.'

They moved back along the hoof prints to where they diverged from the ones left by Harry Conway.

The unknown rider had ridden in from a stand of cottonwood outside the spread of the brasada. Leading their horses Ballard and McCall retraced the tracks. The shooter had returned to the trees and had ridden through them and beyond, out across the empty landscape.

'We keep going we'll end up on Diamond-M range,' McCall observed. 'Other side of those hills.'

They kept riding, covering a few miles before they rode over the low hills and found themselves overlooking the start of the Diamond-M range.

Here the tracks they were following were faint, but they came and returned along the same lines.

'Ain't proof as such,' Ballard said.

'Not for a lawman, or a court,' McCall said.

'Enough for a suspicion.'

McCall leaned forward in his saddle. He was studying the hoof prints. They were much fainter now but still visible to his sharp eyes.

'They ain't heading for home,' he said.

He indicated the direction the tracks were showing. They were not heading across country. The headquarters of the Diamond-M lay a couple of hours away. Yet the tracks were leading in the direction of the range the furthest from home.

McCall followed his partner's pointing finger.

'They're staying on the property line,' he said.

The tracks were running parallel with the Lazy-C border, where the two outfits edged each other.

'Where did that hombre go?' Ballard wondered.

'Easy way to find out.'

Staying on Lazy-C property the Texans rode the line of tracks as they moved. They stayed on that route. It took them to the most extreme edges of the two spreads. The land rose in a series of hogbacks, the landscape rugged and empty save for some scattered trees and patches of brush.

An hour or so later they came off a rough patch of hilly ground and on the Diamond-M side of the line they came in sight of the lonely line shack. They reined in and pulled their horses into the shadows of a stand of trees and brush.

'Interesting,' McCall said as they studied the shack.

There was a small corral tacked on to one side of the building and a lean-to for equipment. And there were numerous hoof prints coming and going from the shack that led in most directions.

4

With the killing of Harry Conway the stakes had been raised high. Yancey Merrick weighed those odds and realized his plans for the Lazy-C were further forward than he had antici- pated. When he had been informed by Rafe Kershaw there had been a moment when Merrick had taken a breath, his mind whirling at the possible repercussions. He didn't give a damn about Conway's actual death. It was something that had been on the cards for some time. But something for the future. Merrick's overall plan for the neighboring spread did include the removal of Henry Conway and his family. Only he would have spared some thought to its implementation. Out and out murder — though drastic — had its uses.

Merrick realized that Ash Boynton

had taken his instruction about getting rid of the Conway family as a direct instruction to go ahead and remove them by the simplest method. Boynton would simply argue he was doing what he was being paid for. The man was a gun for hire. A killing tool who saw things in black and white. Merrick realized he was going to need to explain things in extreme detail to the man.

He slumped in his big leather-bound chair behind his desk, swiveling it around so he could look out the big window. It overlooked the sprawling ranch yard, with its barns and stables. The long bunkhouse. The pole corral that held the horses his crew used. Beyond the yard he could follow the beginnings of Diamond-M land. It stretched as far as the eye could see and further in every direction. Merrick owned it all, but his desire for more meant he needed the range around him. He had already made strides in getting his hands on some of the smaller spreads. Those were the easy ones. They had neither the strength, nor the money to resist. Once Merrick owned them he incorporated them in his growing empire.

The Lazy-C was the stumbling block. In area practically the same as Diamond-M. But it had the advantage of the best water of all the other spreads in the area. Merrick needed that water. He had big herds and they needed constant food and water. He had contracts to fill. Contracts that he had taken money for. Silent partners back east who would eventually be expecting healthy returns on their investments. Merrick intended fulfilling those investments.

And he had another big scheme in motion that was another reason why he needed access to the Lazy-C. Nothing really to do with water and cattle, but as far as Merrick was concerned it stood head and shoulders over everything else. Merrick had plans that would make the basin vitally important. Something for the future. Something that would mark Beecher's Crossing as a place to be counted.

Merrick had made his presence in the area known by his actions. In Beecher's Crossing his money had already bought him into local businesses and he was making sure that with the money his crews spent in the town he had gained support from the stores and the saloons. They wanted the kind of cash his business brought. Merrick had purchased one of the saloons in town. It had been on the brink of closing. With Merrick's money behind it, spent on improving its presence, The Golden Lady had stepped up in the world. Liquor, gambling, women, the saloon had become the center for entertainment in town. It had become known as the unofficial base for the Diamond-M. Merrick accepted it became a little rough at times. He put that down to the high spirits of the cow outfit crews who frequented the place and no one could deny it offered value for money.

All that would be small change when Merrick's main scheme came to fruition.

The arrival of the spur line in town, already well under way, would add to Beecher's Crossing's standing. Once the line reached town, connecting it to the main east/west line the sky was the limit. It would mean the town was no longer an isolated community. Goods and people would be able to reach Beecher's Crossing with relative ease. And with the added plus of large stock yards, the movement of cattle to outlying markets would also improve.

Yancey Merrick was determined to be at the top of the tree. The Diamond-M would dominate and the money he was already making would increase significantly. He intended to have the Diamond-M brand on more than just cattle. It would be the most important company in and around Beecher's Crossing. He would make it happen.

Merrick swung his swivel chair around, away from the window and back to face his desk. He took a long cigar from the box in front of him, snipped off the end and lit it with a Lucifer from the carved holder next to the cigar box. He let the rich aroma of the cigar curl above his head while he organized his thoughts. After a couple of minutes he stood and crossed his office, opened the door and called for Kershaw to join him.

Rafe Kershaw closed the door as he stepped through. He was a tall lean man. His thick hair, dark and neatly cut, framed his strong-boned face. Though he occupied a responsible position in Merrick's company, Kershaw dressed like a regular cowhand albeit one with ample money to spend on his clothing. He followed Merrick across the room and remained standing until his employer took his own seat.

'Boynton has created a problem,' Merrick said. 'He took it on himself to deal with Conway's son. It was going to happen but I wanted to wait a little.

He's jumped the gun in more ways than one.'

Kershaw thought for a moment as he settled in a seat facing Merrick.

'The man did what he thought was expected of him,' he said.

'Like I said, too soon and too damn clumsy.'

'Have to agree on that.' Kershaw moved awkwardly on his seat, not sure what he should say next.

'Ease off, Rafe, I'm not about to bite you.'

Kershaw managed to relax a little. Not completely because he understood the potential problems that could lie ahead.

'So where do we go from here?' he asked.

'Right now there's no real proof the Diamond-M had anything to do with Conway's death. Oh, people can talk and they will, but there isn't a damn thing they can do to point the finger.'

'Henry Conway nigh on accused you.'

Merrick smiled. 'Hell, of course he did. And he'll know we're after getting our hands on the Lazy-C. The man is no fool. He'll make the connection.'

'And you ain't worried?'

'Rafe, he has his wife and daughter to worry about. We'll let that work on him for a while.'

'Whatever you say, boss. What do we do about Boynton?'

'Keep him close to town. The man likes his liquor. Enjoys poker. Let him spend some time at The Golden Lady. Let him win a few hands at the tables. Keep him distracted until I need him for some more work. Just make him understand there are to be no more unexpected incidents. He takes his orders from me, or you.'

'I'll make sure he understands,' Kershaw said. 'You still want that other plan to go ahead? Those three greasy sackers?'

'Sure. That will keep Conway guessing.'

'You still have that meeting with

Orrin Blanchard?'

Merrick smiled for the first time that day. Just thinking about the man gave him purpose. Orrin Blanchard was an important factor in Merrick's upcoming plan for the Diamond-M and the surrounding area.

'Blanchard will be arriving in town later this morning. I want him met and brought directly out here.'

Merrick stood and crossed the room to stand in front of a map pinned to the wall. He gazed at it, nodding to himself as he traced a line with his finger. From the main rail track along the penciled-in line across country that terminated at Beecher's Crossing. When it was built it would connect Beecher's Crossing to the outside world. The township would no longer be isolated. The ninety-odd miles of steel track would bring wealth, commerce, and people to Beecher's Crossing. And Yancey Merrick would be the man who created it. At the top of the heap.

His gaze moved over the map, resting

on the shaded area that represented the Lazy-C. The only setback. The Lazy-C land stood in the way of the spur line. If Merrick couldn't gain ownership of the spread the line would be forced to incorporate a long and time-consuming diversion. Having to do that would push up construction costs dramatically, perhaps even creating a situation where Merrick's dream might have to be ended.

'No easy way around this?' Kershaw asked.

'No,' Merrick said. 'Conway and his damned Lazy-C is the only obstacle in the way. I don't want Blanchard getting a whiff there might be trouble. If he does I could lose his support.'

'But that shouldn't be a problem yet,' Kershaw said. 'Construction is still a long way away. Gives you time to deal with Conway.'

'That's where the problem lies,' Merrick said. 'Time passes faster than you imagine.' He glanced at the wall clock. 'You need to get the buckboard ready and head for town.'

Alone in his office Merrick went to the carved drinks cabinet and poured himself a thick tumbler of whiskey. He stood at the window, watching the activity outside. He swallowed the whiskey with a swift motion.

'You think you have problems now, Conway,' he said. 'Wait until I really get started.'

5

McCall pointed to a line of hoof prints that led from the line shack and across the boundary line. Riders had crossed onto the Lazy-C range and from the condition of the prints not so long ago.

'Appears we have visitors,' he said.

'Why don't we go say hello,' Ballard suggested.

They spurred their mounts, picking up the tracks that ran directly across the Lazy-C range. Coming down to lower ground the Texans were able to spot the riders. Three of them, moving steadily across the grazing land. Beyond the trio groups of Lazy-C cattle could be seen. The steers were contentedly cropping at the grass, paying no mind to the three riders. A few hundred yards further on was one of the large watering holes that dotted the Lazy-C range.

'What the hell are these jokers

playing at?' McCall asked.

His question was answered when one of the riders slid a rifle from its sheath. He raised it, aimed and put a slug in one of the steers. The animal dropped as the slug went in through its skull.

McCall and Ballard kicked their mounts into motion, easing out their own rifles as they cut in towards the three riders.

The man with the rifle was leveling it at a second steer when McCall shouldered his Winchester and triggered a trio of fast shots. He was shooting on the move so his accuracy was not as good as it should have been. Two slugs went wild — the third hit the shooter in the left shoulder, knocking him sideways. The man dropped his rifle as he grabbed for his saddle-horn with his good arm. His partners made attempts to pull their own weapons on target. They were slow. Ballard hit one with a single shot from his Winchester, sending the man from his horse. He landed face down, hard, his body bouncing as he landed. The third man stood up in his stirrups, his rifle hard against his shoulder. He pulled the trigger and sent a shot that burned across the top of McCall's shoulder. Ignoring the hit McCall returned fire, laying in a couple of shots that sent the shooter down.

The echo of the shots died away as the Texans dismounted and approached the scene. McCall sheathed his rifle and took out his Colt. As he approached the man he'd shot in the shoulder he could hear the man cursing wildly as he clutched at his wound. Blood was seeping through his fingers.

'You want to get down off there, mister,' McCall said, keeping the man well covered. 'Climb or fall, don't make no never mind to me.'

Stepping in close McCall pulled the man's handgun from its holster and tossed it clear, then moved aside. While McCall did this Ballard had taken a look at the other two men. When he glanced at his partner Ballard simply shook his head.

'They done for?' the wounded man asked.

'You play rough games,' McCall said, 'so it's no surprise when it deals you a bad hand.'

The man, sliding from his saddle, stared at McCall.

'Sounds to me you don't give a damn my friends are dead.'

'You boys have good intentions when you turned your guns on us?' Ballard asked.

He took a look at the men's horses and the gear they carried behind their saddles.

'Jess, you know what we got here? A damn greasy sack outfit. These yahoos were out to shoot Lazy-C cattle and cut themselves some prime beef.'

He showed his partner the collection of tools, mainly razor-sharp skinning and cutting knives.

Greasy sackers were nothing more than cattle thieves, who took down steers and rode off with the spoils. They carried everything they needed in the burlap sacks. Times were they would ride off with the rustled cattle and sell them wherever they could, but the Texans had come on a trio who were simply there to slaughter and leave the dead cattle where they lay.

'You boys must have been yearning for fresh steaks,' McCall said. 'You working for someone or just yourselves?'

'Ain't got nothin' to say. Anyhows I'm bleeding pretty bad here. I need a doctor.'

The man, lean and gaunt, unshaven, his wild hair hanging over the collar of his grubby shirt, slumped to the ground, legs twisted under him. Despite the pain of his wound he seemed to be showing more interest in the large wrapped bundle behind the saddle of one of the horses.

'What you got there, son?' McCall asked, his own curiosity aroused now.

'Ain't nothin'.'

54

'Now you've got me curious,' McCall said.

He crossed to the horse and unlashed the canvas over the tied-down bundle. A pair of heavy canvas bags were hung over the horse's back. McCall prodded one.

'What's in here?'

The man squirmed under McCall's hard stare.

'Don't know. That's Kiley's horse. I don't know what he brung.'

'Son, you are out and out lying to me,' McCall said. 'I don't like that. You and your partners came to the Lazy-C for more than a side of beef. Now you better tell me else I'm going to make you eat what's in these sacks.'

Ballard took a look at the bags. He pulled on the thick gloves tucked under his belt and loosened the cord tie around the neck of one of them.

'Hope you got an appetite,' McCall said.

'You can't make me . . . ' the man

said, his face pale and greasy with sweat.

'Arsenic powder,' Ballard said. He jerked a thumb in the direction of the watering hole. 'Dump that in the water, the cows drink it and die from arsenic poisoning.'

'That wasn't what we were doing,' the man protested.

'Hell, no, son. Everybody hauls around sacks of arsenic for the fun of it,' McCall said.

He reached down and caught hold of the man's shirt, lifting him bodily to his feet.

'It wasn't me,' the man yelled. 'It was Kiley's idea. All I was here for was the meat.'

'That's good enough to get you hung. Rustling a man's livestock is just as bad as poisoning it.'

'*Hanging*? You can't hang me.'

'Now he's a lawyer,' McCall said. 'This is a talented son of a bitch.'

'I'm hurt,' the man said. 'I'm like to bleed to death out here.'

'You look to him,' Ballard said. 'I'll put these other boys over their saddles and tie 'em down.'

Ignoring the protests and moans of the wounded man McCall did what he could. His slug had gone through and out, leaving a bloody, messy hole. McCall plugged the wound with a wadded piece of the man's shirt, then bound it with more strips to hold it in place.

'Goddam, that's my best shirt,' the man groused.

'Son, I can see that,' McCall agreed. 'Now quit making a fuss else I'll poke that hole with a sharp stick.'

The man glared at him, then decided it wouldn't be in his best interest to upset the big Texan. He fell silent and sat down again. McCall left him to help Ballard with the two dead men.

'Now maybe I'm making a stretch here,' Ballard said, 'but seeing as how these boys came from a Diamond-M line shack, you figure maybe this was all down to our neighbor Merrick?'

McCall thought about it. 'Fits in with the man wanting to make things uncomfortable for the Lazy-C. Another way of sticking the knife in. Something for Ray Bellingham to look into.'

The wounded man said, 'I hear you boys talkin'. It about me?'

'Well, hell, boy,' McCall said, 'what else we even got to talk about? It's all about you.'

Between them Ballard and McCall got the moaning man back on his horse. They collected all the discarded weapons, picked up the dangling reins of the horses and their silent burdens, and moved out.

They had a long ride ahead, across the Lazy-C range to Beecher's Crossing.

'What's your name, feller?' Ballard asked.

'Ain't tellin'. What you need to know for?'

'Only Christian to know a man's name if you going to speak over him.'

The man, riding ahead, twisted in the saddle. 'I ain't dead.'

'Then just hope we don't come across a nice strong tree with a hanging branch on it,' Ballard said.

This got a muttered response, followed by silence.

'I think you hurt his feelings,' McCall said, rubbing his shoulder where the bullet had nipped his skin.

'I'm likely to sleep better tonight knowing that,' Ballard said.

6

Ballard and McCall rode directly to Beecher's Crossing. Two dead men were draped over their saddles, the third man sitting his own saddle in silence. Ballard had done what he could for the man's shoulder. When they reached town the resident doctor would tend to it.

They had been riding for some time when Ballard glanced across at his partner.

'This is getting to be unnerving,' he said.

McCall looked his way. 'What?'

'You haven't said a damn word for the last hour.'

'I been thinking.'

'Even worse.'

'I'm serious, Chet. Had something on my mind a while now.'

'I'm listening.'

'The spreads that sold out. Three outfits. Sitting empty. Vern Bergmann's. Jay Tucker. Then Cy Morrissey.'

'Word has it Merrick bought 'em.'

'That's the part got me thinking. I checked on one of Henry's maps back to home. None of those three are close enough to the Diamond-M to cause him any problems. No real threat. So why'd Merrick feel the need to buy them out?'

'Never give it much thought.'

'I didn't until I did kind of notice something,' McCall said. 'Those three parcels of land sit in a near-enough straight line and when you follow that line the most interesting thing is they all lead to the Lazy-C.'

Ballard took interest then. 'That a fact?'

'It's a fact, partner. I'm just trying to make somethin' out of that.'

When they reached town McCall called in to report what had happened to Ray Bellingham while Ballard carried on to the town doctor's office with the wounded man.

Bellingham arranged for the bodies to be delivered to the undertaker, then made his way to the doctor to be on hand once the wounded man had been dealt with. When that had all been taken care of McCall and Ballard met up on the street.

'Arsenic powder?' the lawman said.

'Drop it in the water and we got a lot of dead cows on the Lazy-C range.'

'Damn sure they weren't carryin' it around to sweeten their coffee,' Ballard said.

'I'll talk to our uncooperative friend,' Bellingham said. 'Let him sweat for a while first until it all sinks in.'

Ballard noticed McCall's restless mood.

'I know you got a burr under your saddle,' he said. 'Spit it out.'

'Damn right I got me an itch I need to scratch,' McCall said. 'Figure I'll take me a ride and check out those empty spreads.'

Ballard grinned at his partner. He walked with him to where they had left their horses. McCall mounted up.

'I'll see you later back at the Lazy-C.'

'Take your time.'

McCall raised a hand and rode out of town.

Marshal Bellingham appeared a little while later, with the wounded man. Ballard fell in alongside and went with Bellingham to the jail. When the prisoner was secured in one of the cells, Ballard shared a mug of coffee with Bellingham as they talked over the current events. Ballard decided it was time he returned to the Lazy-C, said his goodbye and stepped out onto the boardwalk.

'Ballard. Step out here. We got business that won't wait.'

Ballard turned slow and easy. He saw the figure stepping off the boardwalk outside The Golden Lady saloon.

Tall. Bony face. A pair of holstered pistols on his hips. Hands already hovering over them.

Ash Boynton.

'Ballard, you don't have your friends

to back you now. So no walking away this time,' Boynton said. 'I told you your time was coming. We do this here and now.'

Ray Bellingham, who had exited the jail behind Ballard, stepped to the edge of the boardwalk, his hand close to his holstered Colt.

'This is not happening,' he said.

He picked up the movement behind him too late. Felt the twin muzzles of a shotgun press against his spine.

'Stay out of this, lawdog,' Rafe Kershaw said. 'You let those two have their time.'

Ballard took his time turning fully around. He let his right hand hang over his gun as he faced Ash Boynton. Boynton was on the street, facing Ballard. The Texan paced off to confront the man.

'Didn't expect you to face me,' Boynton said.

'I suspect that. Way I figure having your man facing away is more your style,' Ballard said. 'Heard it told more'n once. Makes me remember how Harry Conway died.'

Boynton's nostrils flared as he heard that.

'You work that out all by yourself?'

'I don't hear you deny it.'

'I don't need to. See, Ballard, you need proof.'

Ballard let his gaze drop to the man's feet. Small. Encased in boots with pointed toes.

'You can tell a lot about a man from his tracks,' he said. 'Odd things. Like the size of his feet and the shape of his boots. Like the ones I saw where Harry Conway was killed. Or should say murdered. Shot in the back by a coward . . . '

Ballard knew then that was right. The expression on Boynton's lean face confirmed his thoughts. He was facing Harry Conway's killer. Boynton still displayed the arrogance that was as much a part of him as the air he breathed but there was a trace of fear in his eyes as he faced the Texan.

'Boynton, you just gave me the answer I needed,' Ballard said.

Boynton edged forward. There was a thin film of sweat on his face.

'So?'

'I just wanted you to know I got your cut. And backshooter about covers it.'

Boynton stiffened. His shoulders hunched slightly forward as he set himself.

'Conway was a cinch. You're making it too easy for me,' he said. 'And I ain't forgetting Brookner either.'

Ballard smiled easily. Said, 'There you go then. Two of a kind. We going to talk all day, or get it done?'

The Texan's easy manner threw Boynton off for a thin second, but he was committed now and there was no stepping back.

His hands moved, fingers curling around the butts of the holstered Colts, doing what he had done so many times before, and he began to slide the revolvers free. Fast and smooth as always.

Even Ray Bellingham, watching close,

failed to catch Ballard's move.

He heard the heavy thunder of the shot and saw Boynton step back, a dark hole showing above his left eye. When he switched his gaze to Ballard he was barely in time to see the Texan's gun drop back into his holster.

A burst of red erupted from Boynton's skull as he slumped to his knees, then toppled face down in the street. The back of his head was split open and bloody where the .45 slug had exited.

Bellingham heard Kershaw gasp, thrown by the suddenness of the event. The shotgun barrels withdrew from Bellingham's spine. The Marshal made his own fast draw, pivoted, and before Kershaw could react he whipped the cold steel across the side of Kershaw's head. The Diamond-M hardcase went down, sprawling across the boardwalk. Bellingham took the shotgun and Kershaw's handgun, then stepped back.

Figures were moving on the street, their curiosity piqued as they viewed Boynton's bloody corpse.

'He went for his guns first,' Bellingham said. 'You still outdrew him. I
never knew you were that fast.'

'Not something it's wise to brag
about,' Ballard said.

'How . . . ?'

Ballard held up his right hand. It
shook slightly. He flexed his fingers a
few times and the trembling eased off.

'Comes down to you or the other
feller,' he said. 'I guess wanting to be
the one to walk away makes all the
difference. And remembering what
happened to Harry . . . '

'You near enough got him to admit
he killed Harry.'

'Boynton's kind like to talk.'

Cyrus Makin, Bellingham's part-time
deputy, appeared, his face pale. He was
carrying a Greener, held close to his
chest. The deputy could barely take his
eyes off Ballard.

'I never seen anything like that afore,'
he said.

'With luck you'll never see it again,'
Bellingham said. 'Cyrus, you go fetch

Doc and tell the undertaker to come as well. Now just you go and do that.'

Makin lumbered off along the street.

'Boynton was bound and determined to call this down,' Bellingham said. 'It was a justified shooting, Chet, I'll be witness to that.'

Ballard swept his hat off and ran a hand through his hair.

'Justified, or no,' he said, 'it don't make it any easier. You want my gun, Ray?'

Bellingham gave a shaky laugh. 'Wouldn't feel right even asking for it.'

'What about Kershaw?' Ballard asked.

Bellingham glanced down at the stunned figure sprawled on the board-walk.

'He's got a stretch in a cell coming. Armed assault against an officer of the law.'

'He got off light,' Ballard said, glancing at Boynton's body. 'You need me to sign any paperwork, 'cause if not I believe I'll go get me a drink over to the Quarter Horse Saloon.'

7

McCall had ridden for a few hours. A steady pace that covered the miles and drew him away from Beecher's Crossing and the Lazy-C. He rode empty land. For the most part wide and untouched. Not exactly barren, but showing no signs of habitation, or even a suggestion of it. Ahead, hazy in the heat, he made out a range of low hills that crossed his path. It took him another hour before he saw the wide, rocky cut in the hills. A way through. Drawing closer he saw the cut was around sixty feet wide and as far as he could see it extended deep into the slopes. McCall guessed it would extend all the way through the hills to the far side. When he rode in, the rocky walls rising on either side, the sound of his horse's hooves echoed around him. He rode for at least two miles before the cut ended and he emerged on the far side to yet another open landscape. A gentle slope lay ahead, flattening out after a hundred feet where it met the open flatland.

Open but not empty. A half-mile further on were men and machinery. Activity that confirmed the thoughts that had been crowding McCall's mind and brought him all the way out here to confirm his suspicions.

He was looking at a railhead camp. McCall drew rein and sat studying the site. It didn't take him long to realize what he was looking at. It was a track-laying outfit. A gang of workers, piles of steel rails and wooden ties. Equipment. A number of tents and an open kitchen with a fire under cooking pots. Behind the camp, on rails that had already been laid, was a steaming locomotive, with a couple of box cars attached. He didn't need Conway's maps to tell him where the track was intended to be laid.

It was heading for Beecher's Cross-ing.

And the Lazy-C lay directly ahead of the track.

McCall sighed. Things were really starting to make some kind of sense. The pressure being put on Henry Conway. Anything and everything to get him to relinquish his ownership of the land. It looked to McCall that it was because the Lazy-C would lie in the direct path of the line. If it had to go around the Lazy-C the costs and the circumstances of rerouting the track would put up the overall expenses and also add to the time it would take. McCall was no expert on the complexities of the business, but he was pretty certain he'd heard of penalty clauses attached to contracts. If the track-laying was held up the investors would face heavy charges.

He could understand now why Merrick might be in such a hurry to gain control of the Lazy-C. It was plain to see he was connected to the building of the rail line. McCall ventured a guess that Merrick was involved up to his neck. Had most likely made a deal with the rail company that involved getting the Lazy-C out of the way so the construction could go ahead without delay.

McCall put his horse down the slope, heading for the camp site. He made no attempt to hide his presence, though as he rode he eased the Winchester in the saddle boot and slipped the hammer loop free on his holstered Colt. No harm in being prepared. As he neared the camp McCall couldn't fail to notice a small number of loitering men who were by no stretch rail workers. They were gunhands. He could see that from the way they were dressed, wearing their holstered handguns openly tied down. He saw a number of them turn and watch him close. That didn't bother him. Jess McCall had quit being worried about hard stares and scowls a long time ago. He simply eased his horse into camp and reined in near the cook fires.

'Was wondering if a man could get a

cup of coffee seeing as how you got a hell of a pot there,' he said, an amiable expression on his face.

'This ain't no church social handout,' a hulking man said. 'I don't see no sign saying we pass out free coffee to every saddle tramp who rides by.'

'Well forgive me to all get out,' McCall said. 'I was just passing by and saw your camp. Thought maybe I'd ask polite like. Been a long day. Now I might not be dressed in my Sunday best but saddle tramp is kind of harsh.'

The man moved a little closer, hooking thick thumbs in his belt. He wore his strapped-down revolver like it was a banner showing itself to the world in general. McCall had to admit the man was big. In every direction. Muscle showed. Not fat. He stared at McCall, screwing up his unshaven face as the sun hit it. McCall decided he didn't really care for the fellow, him being all impolite.

'You look like a tramp to me.'

'Hell, son, I ain't about to argue with

a man of your intellect.'

This time the man made a sound deep in his throat.

'See, mister, I don't know you and that worries me.'

McCall considered that. 'Hell, son, I don't know you either — so I guess we're sort of even.'

The big man's scowl stretched across his face. McCall saw his shoulder muscles tense as if he was about to do something.

Then a voice broke through the strained silence.

'Ease off there, fellers. We don't want any hassle.'

The speaker planted himself between the big man and McCall's horse. He was tall and blond, his face browned from a life in the outdoors. Ladies would have called him handsome. His pants were expensive and well cut, his shirt tailored, sleeves rolled up and the collar unbuttoned. The half-boots he wore were custom-made.

'I'm Bruce Collhurst. I ramrod this

outfit. Heard you were looking for a cup of coffee. Step down.' Collhurst waved a hand at a man wearing a cook's apron. 'Jenks, fetch this man a mug.'

He smiled and the expression was reflected in his gray eyes. He held out a strong hand and took McCall's as he dismounted.

McCall stretched the kinks out of his back and took the enamel mug that was handed to him.

'Jess McCall,' he said.

'Pay no heed to Mister Bell,' Collhurst said. 'He's naturally suspicious of anyone who doesn't work for the company. Can't blame him, though. It's part of his job to make sure we don't have unwelcome visitors.'

McCall tasted the strong, hot coffee, watching Mister Bell as he did, and receiving a continued dark look from the man. He judged Bell to be a shade over six-foot-six, which made him McCall's height. Bell was also extremely broad across his shoulders and chest. McCall made a mental note of that just in case matters became unfriendly.

'He earns his pay then,' McCall said.

Collhurst gave a low chuckle. 'He does that all right.'

'Believe it, bucko,' Bell muttered as he moved away. 'And don't doubt I'll not forget you.'

McCall made a point of ignoring the man.

'You from these parts?' Collhurst asked.

McCall decided that playing the innocent might work in his favor. Took his time, swallowing more coffee before he spoke.

'I'm passing through. Heard there might be jobs on offer at a big spread along the ways. Diamond-M I was told. Figured to go check it out. You heard of it?'

'Only by name,' Collhurst said. 'You're a long way from the main line.'

'Spurline. Going to lay track to the town along the way. Country around here is growing. There's a need to open things up. Get people connected.'

'I heard laying track can be a tough job.'

'All part of the business. Rain, shine, hard or soft, we get through one way or the other. We don't turn aside for anything.' He paused. 'Or anyone.'

McCall emptied his coffee. Ran a big hand over his face.

'Hope I never have to stand in your way,' he said. 'Get the feeling you'd ride straight over me. This town, it got a name?'

'Beecher's Crossing. Line may go on further if things work out. Mind we still got a long way to go. Going to be a couple of months before we get as far as Beecher's Crossing.'

McCall handed his mug to the cook. 'Obliged, friend.'

He went to mount up. Saw Bell still eyeing him from a distance.

'Tell Mister Bell I said goodbye.'

'I'll do that. You ride easy, McCall.'

'I always do.' He settled in his saddle. 'Good luck,' he said.

'I make my own luck,' Collhurst said, smiling, but this time the smile failed to reach his eyes.

He stood watching McCall ride away. He sensed movement close by. It was Bell. The big man folded his powerful arms across his chest.

'Something on your mind, Cleve?'

'I don't trust that hombre. More to him than just a passing cowboy. Could be he's doing some snooping with a mind to put out the word on us.'

'Had to happen sooner or later,' Collhurst said. 'I believe you could be right. So let's keep our eyes open. Have your boys ride a wide loop. In case Mister McCall is more than he pretends to be.'

Bell grunted an acknowledgement and walked over to where his men were gathered.

★　★　★

McCall knew he was being watched as he left. He made a point of not looking back. Calling on the camp had told him what he needed to know.

The rails were being laid in the direction of town. The Lazy-C lay between the tracks and Beecher's Crossing. Collhurst had made it clear he was not going to deviate from the plans. Which meant he was going to cross Conway's land. That was not a good sign for the Lazy-C. Railroad companies had a reputation for forging their way regardless. It had happened before as expansionism bulldozed across the country. There was power behind the railroads. Power that could include political clout and high finance. The line intended to open up Beecher's Crossing might not stand tall compared to the transcontinental lines, but it would still create wealth and offer opportunities to those who were determined to push it through. The ninety-odd miles from the main line to Beecher's Crossing would bring in more investment. Open up the town and consolidate the businesses and the building of stockyards would give the ranches the chance to ship out their beef rather than have to undergo the long drives that took time and a great deal of manpower.

He had been riding for close on an hour when he caught a glimpse of a rider in the distance, off to his left, moving parallel to his line of travel. McCall didn't make a definite show of noticing the rider. He kept going. Ahead of him the way merged with a stretch of timbered and rocky terrain. The land stretched across his path in both directions and there was no way around it.

'Seems to me, hoss,' he said quietly, 'we likely rattled someone back there. Enough so they want to take a closer look at us.'

He took his horse into the timber, letting it find its way. Once he was in the shadowed closeness McCall slid his Winchester free and laid it across his thighs. A latticework of shadow from the sun lancing through the trees made it harder to spot the trailing rider, but McCall did catch a glimpse of the man, still following and now angling in towards McCall.

'This could go on all damn day,' McCall said.

* * *

He was becoming restless. Having someone dogging his trail did not sit well with the Texan. So he decided to push the game forward. He spotted a mass of tumbled rocks ahead, moss-covered along one side, and large enough to hide him as he passed. The second his horse took him alongside the rocks McCall slid his feet from the stirrups and stepped from the saddle and onto the lower rocks, quickly moving up the rising slope of higher boulders. As he cleared the uppermost rocks he dropped to a crouch, the Winchester in both hands. Looking over the curve McCall was able to see down the far side.

The rider trailing him was partway along the rock formation, leaning forward in his saddle. The man held a long-barreled revolver in his right hand as he guided his mount with his left.

'Let the gun go,' McCall said, leveling the Winchester. 'I won't ask a second time. And you can take that as read.'

The rider picked up where the voice was coming from and jerked his head up. McCall recognized him as one of the men Bell had been talking with at the railhead camp.

The man stared at McCall's rifle, weighing his chances. Then he muttered under his breath and let the Remington drop from his hand.

'And the long gun.'

The man slid his rifle from the saddle boot and dropped it.

'Bell couldn't let it go,' McCall said. 'He has a suspicious nature.'

'What did he want you to do?'

'It wasn't to hand you an invite to supper.'

'Glad to hear that 'cause I'm particular who I eat with.'

'And you got something against the railroads?'

'Hell, son, I rode on many a train in my time. I just don't like the way things tend to get tetchy once you fellers start laying down those rails.'

The man shrugged his shoulders. 'It's the way it is. You buck Collhurst you bring trouble down on your head. He's the kind who doesn't back down.'

'At least we have that in common.'

'What do we do now?'

'You turn that pony around and go back the way you came.'

'What about my guns?'

'I'll leave them with Marshal Bellingham in town. You can pick them up from there if you ever get that far.' McCall could see the man was having a problem, but he didn't give a damn about that. 'Son, my patience is wearing thin. Just get out of my sight.'

The man snatched up his reins and pulled his horse around. McCall watched him go, waiting until the man had cleared the timber and was out in the open where he could keep an eye on him. He slid down off the rocks and picked up the discarded weapons, went and fetched his own horse where it had stopped and waited for him. He jammed the Remington in his saddle-bag and the rifle in his own boot, keeping his Winchester in his hands. Back in the saddle McCall sat and watched the distant rider until he vanished behind a ridge, then turned about and continued his journey back to the Lazy-C.

8

In the ranch kitchen Henry Conway sat at the head of the big table, his hands spread flat on the scrubbed wood. Helen busied herself with making fresh coffee, while Chris put hot biscuits on a plate.

McCall stood at the far end of the table, hat in hand. Laney Chancery sat to one side.

'So now we know,' Conway said. 'Merrick wants the Lazy-C so they can push this spurline across to reach town.'

'Seems to me he wants the spread and the right of way,' Chancery said.

Chris banged a plate down on the table, her young face flushed with anger.

'Well, he won't get either,' she said fiercely. 'Not without a fight.'

Helen Conway placed mugs of coffee in front of everyone. McCall couldn't help noticing the way her hands trembled as she carried the mugs. He took one from her.

'Go sit down, ma'am,' he said.

'Thank you, Jess.'

Chancery fiddled with his mug.

'Henry, he can't just walk in and lay his tracks across the Lazy-C.'

Conway's face gave away his thoughts and he gave a slight shake of his head.

'Man staked his claim by building his house and settin' down roots. He held his land by working it. By taking up arms against anyone who tried to steal it from him. That's what I did. Same as any man around here.'

'Merrick will use the strength of the railroad company. He'll turn every trick in the book,' McCall said.

'I need to talk with George Sutton,' Conway said. 'Make sure our legal standing holds firm.'

'Dad, the Lazy-C has title to this land,' Chris said. 'Merrick, or the rail company, can't just steal from us.'

'Henry, whatever you decide, the crew will stand behind you,' Chancery said. 'This ain't no time to let ourselves be caught off guard.'

'Jess, will you ride with me to town? Let's get this sorted.'

When Conway had made his way from the kitchen, with Chancery on his heels, Helen said, 'Stay with him, Jess. He'll work himself into a stubborn mood and when he does . . . '

'I won't let him do himself any harm.'

'This isn't going to go away quietly,' Chris said. 'It's already gone too far.'

'You ladies stay close to home,' McCall said. 'You've got the Lazy-C crew to watch over you. I'll keep Henry safe.'

* * *

'How did I let this happen?' Conway said.

He and McCall were on the way to Beecher's Crossing. They had left the ranch well behind them but not the tense mood that had settled over the outfit. McCall had always seen Conway as a solid, resistant man. To build a brand like the Lazy-C took strength and purpose. Much of that had been knocked out of Conway with the death of his son. He seemed to be lacking some of that inner strength right now.

'You didn't let it happen,' McCall said. 'Merrick and his partners forced it. Figured they could deal their hand without anyone knowing. Now we do know we make sure they can't win.'

It was late afternoon when McCall and Conway reached town. While Conway went to speak with lawyer Sutton, McCall tied his horse outside Bellingham's office. He took the rifle and pistol and went inside. The Marshal was behind his desk, busy with paperwork. The moment McCall appeared he pushed back from the desk, obviously glad for an excuse to take a break.

'Jess.'

He watched as McCall placed the rifle and handgun on his desk.

'You might have the owner coming in to collect these.'

'You take them away from him?'

'Didn't want to leave him the temptation to use them.'

McCall told the story of his visit to the rail camp and his discussion with Bruce Collhurst and Cleve Bell. He finished by telling about the man who had trailed him from the camp.

'Rail camp? Damnation,' Bellingham said. 'I can see this boiling up into a big mess.'

'Henry is over at his lawyer's office right now looking into the legal side of things. Ray, he doesn't want trouble, but he also isn't going to stand by and watch Merrick and the railroad move in.'

'He could have a fight on his hands like it or not. I've heard of Collhurst. Hard as they come. He's railroad all the way through. And the man uses the law as well. Railroad has its own lawyers to stand behind anything Collhurst does. And they'll be siding with Merrick.'

'So Collhurst and Merrick are both playing their hands.'

Bellingham nodded. 'Had Merrick's local lawyer in yesterday. Standing bail for Rafe Kershaw.' When McCall registered interest Bellingham said, 'Won't have heard I guess? Ash Boynton called Chet out. They went at it and Boynton ended up with one of Chet's bullets in him. Clear case of self defense. When it kicked off Kershaw stuck a shotgun in my back to keep me out of it. Had to buffalo him when it was over. Tossed him in a cell to wait on Judge Henshaw's convenience. Only thing the Judge is out of town and I figured Kershaw out of jail takes the pressure off. Last thing I need is a bunch of Merrick's yahoos making more trouble.'

'What about our friend with the arsenic?'

'He ain't talking. I took a sneaky look after I locked Kershaw up. Now that pair were pretending awful hard they didn't know each other. Pretending too hard. Interesting thought, when I went through the gear those three were carrying. They each had a hefty roll of cash in their saddlebags. For greasy sackers they were well heeled. Don't make much sense they were supposed to be dirt poor but holding big money behind their saddles.'

'Interesting,' McCall said.

'Ain't it just.'

'Where's Chet?'

'Haven't seen him today. Last I spoke to him he was heading for the Quarter Horse for a drink. Come to think it's unusual for Chet to get himself lost.'

'He wasn't at the Lazy-C. That's where I rode in from. And didn't see him on the road either.'

The news concerned McCall. It wasn't in Ballard to simply up and disappear.

'So where is he?'

9

Ballard was trying to figure that out himself. It didn't help that he had a sullen headache from having a gun barrel bent over his skull. When he gingerly touched the back of his skull he felt the raised welt there, with crusted blood that told him he had been unconscious for some time. He was stretched out on a dirty floor. He took a look at his surroundings. He was in some kind of storehouse. A dusty, untidy place that smelled of leather and old sacking. He also realized he was not tied up. His arms and legs were free. He heard movement. It came from the other side of the storehouse door. Ballard could see light shining through the gaps in the door and when he checked he saw dusty sunbeams angling in through the walls.

The bitter part was him walking into

it with both eyes wide open. The shootout with Boynton had soured Ballard's mood. The pure fact that Boynton had pushed the matter made no difference. He left Ballard with little choice. And the near admission that Boynton had bushwhacked Harry Conway only added to the situation. Caught out, Boynton had let himself slip. Yet even with the revelation the gunman had been unable to fully conceal his guilt. Like all men who lived by the gun Ash Boynton had to crow. It was the mark of a killer. The admission of what he felt was something to brag about. And once he had let slip his involvement, there was no way back for him. Boynton's reputation as a fast and deadly shootist meant he had to maintain that persona.

After the confrontation Ballard, feeling subdued, had taken himself off to the saloon and had downed a couple of drinks. Not exactly feeling sorry for himself, but reflecting on how the situation centered around the Lazy-C seemed to be escalating. Later, realizing he was not doing anything to resolve matters, he had walked out of the saloon. His mind was still occupied when he reached the livery stable and went out back to catch up his horse.

He recalled sensing movement close by. Shadowed figures closing in. He had turned to see who it was. Too slow and too late. The figures came at him in a rush. Hands reaching out to grasp at his clothing. Pulling. Tugging him off balance.

And then the unexpected slam of something hard crashing down across the back of his skull. The blow darkened his world and Ballard had no strength or will to fight it. He went down . . . into a terrible silence, devoid of light and of awareness . . .

Ballard knew without having to look that his handgun was gone, leaving an empty holster. With that discovery he knew his knife would be gone as well.

No gun. No knife. Whoever had

taken him had made sure he wouldn't have any weapons to be able to fight with. They had left him defenseless. Or so they thought. It was their first mistake and if Ballard had any say in the matter it would turn out to be their last.

He was curious as to why he'd been pistol whipped and dragged off somewhere. He might not have any details but he was certain sure it had to do with the Lazy-C problem. Unless it was something personal. His shootout with Boynton? Maybe Boynton's friends looking for payback? He didn't dismiss the possibility. That reminded Ballard of Rafe Kershaw. He had ridden with Boynton. Was he out to avenge the man? If that was the case why hadn't Kershaw simply killed him once he had Ballard at a disadvantage?

Ballard stopped right there. Too much thinking was making his head ache even worse. He slowly climbed to his feet, careful not to make too many hasty movements. Crossing to the door

Ballard peered through the gaps in the planks. He could see a section of an empty yard. No sound, no movement. Squinting his eyes sideways he made out the corner of a larger building and a run-down, empty corral. What he saw offered him no more information. On impulse Ballard tried the door. It creaked but refused to open.

He took another look around. There was nothing he could use as a weapon. Ballard squeezed his fists together, hearing his knuckles pop. At least he still had the use of his hands.

He paced back and forth. Restless. Trying to figure how long he'd been in the shed. From the brightness of the day he guessed it must be close to, or just past, noon. By now someone must be wondering where he was. A man just didn't go missing without it being noticed.

He knew that once McCall realized he was gone he would start looking. And being McCall that could amount to a lot of grief if he didn't get the answers he wanted. McCall wasn't a man who had patience for unanswered questions.

And when Jess McCall became dissatisfied life could turn hectic.

That was often more than most people could handle.

10

Jess McCall stood outside the jail, fingers hooked in his belt, staring along main street. He was working on the information he'd learned about his partner. The final piece told him the last place Ballard had mentioned was the saloon halfway along the street.

The Quarter Horse.

That was what Bellingham had heard.

McCall decided it was as good a place to start as any. He sensed someone moving alongside. It was Ray Bellingham. The Marshal had followed McCall's gaze.

'You thinking about calling in there?'

'Might be able to find out where Chet went when he walked out. Can't hurt to ask.'

'Ask for Milt Lander. He owns the place. Milt's a good man. You'll get the truth from him. Jess, I'll be around.'

McCall nodded and stepped off the boardwalk, taking a slow walk up the street. As he neared the saloon he saw Henry Conway on the far side of the street, passing the time of day with people he knew. That, McCall decided, was how Beecher's Crossing seemed. A nice town going about its business, with most folk having no idea what was going on around them — or what was heading their way. McCall just had the feeling the inhabitants of Beecher's Crossing were close to having problems explode in their faces.

He reached the boardwalk and went in through the swing doors. Inside it was shady and a few degrees cooler out of the sun. McCall took off his hat and took a moment to look around.

He counted around a dozen patrons. Half at the long, polished bar, the rest scattered around the tables. He crossed to the bar and leaned his elbows on the surface. There were two men behind the bar. A tall, skinny man with a long face and hardly any hair on his head. Closer was a man in his forties. Solid, his graying hair thick, with long sideburns and a heavy mustache. He glanced in McCall's direction and nodded.

'Get you anything?'

'A beer would be nice,' McCall said.

The man went to work filling a thick glass and placed it in front of McCall.

'You'd be Milt Lander?'

'Owner operator,' the man said.

'Got your name from Ray Bellingham.'

'I get the feeling there's a question on its way.'

'You know my partner Chet Ballard?'

'Yeah. He was in here.' Lander took a slow look at McCall. 'There a problem?'

'Looks to have disappeared. He here on his own?'

'I heard about the shootout with Ash Boynton. Soon after Chet came in looking to have himself a drink and a quiet time by himself.'

McCall took a long swallow of beer. 'He talk to anyone?'

Lander shook his head. 'Not helping much, huh?'

'You can only tell what you know,' McCall said.

'Now I understand the problems Henry is having, what with his boy being killed and all. I'm no friend of Yancey Merrick, or the bunch who hang around with him . . . '

McCall sensed there was more to come. 'Anything, Milt.'

'Couple of Merrick's boys showed their faces while Chet was sitting with his drink. Lucas Connor and Bob Yost. When they saw Chet they turned about and left. Now I ain't sayin' that means anything. But what made them skedaddle the minute they set eyes on Chet?'

McCall drained his glass. Dropped some coins on the bar.

'Maybe I'll go and ask them.'

'You walk easy around that pair,' Milt said. 'And don't show 'em your back.'

'Like that, huh?'

'Like that.'

'Where would I find them?'

'They frequent The Golden Lady. Merrick's base when he's in town since he bought it.'

'Thanks, Milt.'

'Careful if you go in there,' Lander said. 'That place doesn't treat strangers too well.'

'I'll remember that, Milt.'

Lander watched the tall Texan leave and wished him well.

★   ★   ★

McCall eased his Colt in the holster, making sure the hammer-loop was clear. He checked the street. Watched a freight wagon rattle its way past, heading for the warehouse section of town. A few riders made their way back and forth. Nothing out of the ordinary. He made his way towards The Golden Lady.

The big saloon had a gaudy frontage.

A bright painted sign. Windows with large lettering. It advertised what it was. A place where men could drink and gamble. Find the company of a friendly girl. McCall had nothing against that, except in this case the saloon had become Yancey Merrick's base in town. As he stepped across the boardwalk McCall picked up the tinny sound of a badly tuned piano.

When he pushed his way through the door and into the saloon McCall's eyes took in the layout. Long bar to his left. It ran the length of the room. A mirror filled the back wall, sleeves holding bottles and cigar cases. There must have been near a couple of dozen tables spread around. Along the opposite side of the saloon were gambling tables. The piano was there as well, a tubby man in shirt sleeves held up by suspenders banging away at the keys.

McCall counted no more than a half-dozen customers spread around the room. A light haze of tobacco smoke drifted overhead. Lamps had been lit against the oncoming dusk.

He made his way to the bar where the lone man on duty watched his progress. He was a large man, dark hair slicked back and shiny, his big hands laid flat on the bar top.

'Lookin' for couple of fellers,' McCall said conversationally. 'Lucas Connor and Bob Yost.'

McCall was looking across the bartender's shoulder as he spoke, watching for any reaction from the customers reflected in the mirror.

'Never heard of 'em,' the bartender said too quickly, his gaze flicking nervously.

McCall saw movement at one of the tables behind him and to his left. There were two men seated there and McCall saw one of them push back his chair and lunge to his feet, left hand reaching for the pistol holstered on his hip. His partner slid awkwardly from his scat, dropping to a crouch, a yell forming on his lips.

McCall turned, clearing his Colt and

leveled it at the left-hand shooter. A pair of shots thundered loudly in the saloon. McCall felt the solid thump of the slug as it hit the bar on his right side. Then his own shot hit home, the lead .45 caliber bullet hammering into his target, high in the chest. The man gave a stunned grunt, twisting halfway round from the impact. He toppled face down across the table, sending bottle and glasses flying, before sliding to the floor. In the couple of seconds following McCall swiveled his body around and picked up on the second man. He was almost on his knees, his move hampering his chance to find a clear target. He was blocked by the table and his drawn gun was almost hidden. He fired in haste and his bullet flew well clear of its intended target, smashing into the mirror behind the bar. The glass shattered and fell with a crash. He fired a second time and failed to hit McCall, who pushed his gun forward and fired through the top of the table, then triggered twice more. Wood splinters exploded from the table as the heavy slugs burned through and found the crouching figure. The man gave a pained cry as already deformed slugs hit him. He took the shots in his shoulder, lurching upright, gun forgotten as he felt the shock of his wounds course through him. He fell back into the seat he had vacated and clutched at his badly bleeding shoulder.

The piano fell silent.

The saloon was suddenly very quiet.

Behind McCall the bartender shuffled to one side.

'No need for you to move,' McCall said. 'Just pretend you forgot about that scattergun you got there 'cause I still have two shots in the pot. You're too big a target to miss and I ain't forgot you said you didn't know these boys.'

McCall moved forward and stepped around the table to hold his Colt on the shoulder-shot man. He stared up at McCall, sheer terror in his eyes. The hand held tight over his messed-up shoulder was wet with blood.

'You need the doc,' McCall said, stating the obvious.

'You going to send for him?'

'If I get the right answer to a question,' McCall said. 'Otherwise we can just wait until you bleed to death.'

The man stared at McCall like he couldn't believe what he had just heard.

'What . . . ?'

'Where's Ballard? And don't pretend you have no idea.'

'Son of a bitch.'

'Ain't I just. And you're still bleeding pretty fast. Right now you need to figure if the pay you're taking is worth dying for.'

The man debated that. Made a quick decision to cooperate because money was of no use to him if he bled to death on the saloon floor.

A couple of minutes later the bartender was on his way to summon the town doctor. He passed Ray Bellingham who had heard the shooting and was heading for The Golden Lady. Bellingham was carrying a Greener.

Customers were starting to slip out

through the door. They flowed around Bellingham as he stood there. When he walked inside the saloon was empty save for the piano player motionless on his stool and a pair of the hostesses standing against the empty bar.

There was a body on the floor beside one of the tables. A bottle and broken glasses near him.

A second man, one shoulder bloody, slumped in a chair.

And Jess McCall standing over him.

'This is starting to be a habit,' Bellingham said, lowering the shotgun. 'I'm getting the feeling you have something against Merrick's crew.'

McCall stepped away from the wounded man, facing Bellingham.

'Those two were the ones who grabbed Chet. Feller with the bullet in his shoulder, Yost, told me where they have him. Doc's on his way.'

'Tell me they did it on Merrick's orders.'

'Rafe Kershaw so it's as good as.'

Bellingham shook his head. 'This is

all getting out of hand, Jess.'

'Merrick is set on pushing his railroad deal through,' McCall said. 'Come hell or high water. And he wants the way open so he can cut across the Lazy-C.'

The town doctor came into the saloon, the bartender behind him. He saw the shot man and went directly to him, shaking his head.

'This used to be a nice, quiet town,' he said.

He put his black bag on the floor and bent over the wounded man.

'I need to go and talk to Henry,' McCall said.

Bellingham noticed the urgency in his voice.

'You better tell me the rest.'

'Yost said something about Chris Conway being in danger. He was only too willing to talk when I told him I wouldn't let the doc tend him until he gave me what I wanted.'

'Then you'd better get moving. I'll deal with Yost.'

* ★ *

McCall cut across country. He had parted company with Henry Conway once they were clear of town. Conway was heading back to the Lazy-C and his family. McCall was searching for his partner. When he had told Conway what he'd learned the man's face paled.

'You believe that?' he asked.

'I figure Merrick is bound and determined to have that railroad push through. He's in deep and won't back down. Henry, he wants the Lazy-C for a right of way. It's why he's been clearing the way taking over those other spreads. I did some checking. Bergmann's place. Jay Tucker. Morrissey's Tumbling-M. Every last one sits along the line the tracks will take. The Lazy-C is the last one.'

'And I'm too big to scare easy,' Conway said.

'So they hit you harder.'

'Murdering my boy is the biggest mistake they could ever make,' Conway said. 'Now they threaten my daughter. Make Chet disappear.'

'Henry, get to home. The Lazy-C has protection for Chris. Chancery and the crew will watch out for her.'

Conway nodded. 'Find Chet,' he said.'

★　★　★

It was full dark when McCall drew rein in an untidy clump of trees and brush. He tied his horse, took his rifle and crouched in the deep shadow as he surveyed the Morrissey place. The sprawl of buildings had taken on a desolate look since the place had been abandoned. Grass and weeds had already taken hold. A couple of poles had dropped out of place in the corral fence. Though it was night there was a good moon casting cold light over the area.

A thin trail of smoke rose from the chimney of the small main house and a pair of horses stood where they had been tied near the water trough next to the corral. A third horse, rope tied, occupied the corral. The moment he set eyes on it McCall recognized it as Ballard's.

'Well that gives the game away,' McCall muttered.

He eased out of cover, taking a wide loop as he approached the house, coming in from the rear. When he flattened against the back wall he could hear muffled voices coming from inside the house. Two voices, equaling the pair of horses he'd seen. McCall decided to move around to the front door, stepping carefully over the scattered rubbish that had been dumped over the years. He made it to the front corner when he heard the house door open.

'You get that coffee poured, Lew, while I go take a look at our guest.'

Leaning out from the corner of the house McCall saw a long-legged man in range clothes emerging from the house. He wore a holstered handgun.

As he pulled the door shut the man

made a casual gesture, his right hand touching the butt of his weapon.

Before he took a step McCall came around the corner of the house, swinging the Winchester round in a brutal arc that slammed across the back of the man's skull. The sound it made was hard and meaty and the man belly-flopped to the ground. He jerked a couple of times before he became still and by this time McCall had moved to the door, raising a booted foot to kick it in. The door crashed open, McCall following and coming face to face with the second man who turned away from the stove where he was reaching for the blackened pot simmering on top of it.

'*Who the hell . . .* '

The man snatched out the Colt he wore, fingers clamping around the butt as he lifted the weapon with lightning speed. The way he handled the gun told McCall he was dealing with an experienced hand, so he didn't hesitate when he triggered the Winchester from hip level. The crash of the shot was loud in the confines of the house, the .44–40 slug catching the man in the left hip, tearing through to shatter bone and macerate flesh. The man fell back, clutching at the hot stove as he hit against it and suffering a burn to his hand. Yelling in pain and anger the man still maneuvered the Colt in his right hand, firing off a single shot that flipped off McCall's hat. The Texan angled the .44–40 and put a second slug in the man, this time in his chest. The man went down hard, gasping against the oncoming pain in his body before he simply became still.

McCall picked up the discarded gun and threw it across the floor. He snatched up his hat, fingering the hole in the brim. He didn't like to think how close it had been. Back outside he briefly checked the inert figure of the first man. The back of the skull was caved in and showed split bone under the blood.

McCall stood in the middle of the

ranch yard, staring around. He saw the tack hut on the far side and walked in that direction.

'*Chet*,' he called. 'You hear me?'

Ballard's voice came from the hut and McCall crossed over and shot the bolts holding the door secure. Ballard stepped out.

'That shooting down to you?'

McCall nodded. 'Couple fellers over to the house. Had to bushwhack one and shoot the other.' He saw Ballard touch a hand to the back of his head. 'You okay?'

'Apart from one hell of a headache.'

They trailed back across the yard. Ballard eyed the man McCall had gun-whipped, then went inside the house and searched for his weapons. When he came back out, buckling on his recovered gunbelt, McCall was on his way to the corral to free Ballard's horse. Ballard had found his hat inside the house and he slapped the dust from it as he joined his partner.

'How did you find me?'

'Had words with Conway and Yost back in town. Managed to persuade Yost to talk. Seems Rafe Kershaw arranged to have you grabbed to keep you out the way.'

Ballard checked his rifle was still sheathed at his saddle. He settled his hat firm, wincing when it brushed the sore spot.

'I can tell you got something else to say,' he said.

'There was talk from Yost about a threat against Chris Conway,' he said.

Ballard was leading his horse as they made their way to collect McCall's animal.

'Sonofabitch,' Ballard said. 'Merrick is really bucking for trouble.'

'When I rode out to find you Henry was on his way back to the Lazy-C to make sure Chris was alright.'

When they were mounted up they cut away from the silent spread and headed back for the Lazy-C.

So much was happening that seemed out of their control. One thing after another. All involving people they knew and cared for. And as Ballard had said it appeared that Yancey Merrick was the man behind it all.

11

'You sleep well?' Merrick asked his guest. It was mid-morning of the following day and Merrick had allowed Orrin Blanchard to sleep late after his long journey from back east.

'Yes,' Blanchard said. 'Extremely well.'

Merrick had been up for hours, seeing to the routine business of the Diamond-M. A ranch as large as his took a firm hand to operate and Merrick was no slouch when it came to handling matters.

'You sure you don't want breakfast?'

'After that meal last night I'm sure. I'll take some of that whiskey you offered me. Never too early for that.'

Yancey Merrick handed a thick tumbler to Orrin Blanchard. The man took it in his big hand and held it up to the light, studying the mellow, amber whiskey with a connoisseur's eye. He sniffed the contents, a soft murmur of appreciation rising from his throat. Taking a sip he rolled the liquid around his mouth before he swallowed.

'Very nice,' he said in his throaty tone. 'I will not stoop and compare it to a beautiful woman because that would be crass. They are two completely different things. Suffice it to say, Yancey, that your taste in whiskey cannot be faulted.'

Blanchard tilted the glass and drained it.

'Another?' Merrick asked.

'Need you ask?'

Blanchard waited until he had the refill in his hand, settling back in the comfortable armchair that faced the window behind Merrick's desk.

Orrin Blanchard was a big man in every way. Big but by no means obese. Standing he was near six foot tall, with powerful shoulders and chest. Little of the flesh that adorned his frame was fat. He was solid. A shade less than handsome, his mobile face showed the inner strength he possessed. Fifty years old, his fair hair was thick on his head and reaching his collar. He studied the world through surprisingly clear blue eyes, intelligence lurking behind them. He was clean-shaven, his mouth wide showing large teeth.

Blanchard was dressed, for him, conservatively in a finely cut white shirt, open-necked, and dark gray pants pulled over polished flat-heeled half-boots. A hand-tooled leather belt showing a heavy silver buckle.

'You really have an impressive home, my boy. Befitting a man of your standing,' he said.

His voice held a trace of his Southern heritage, pronouncing his words with a tempered drawl.

'I like to think so, Orrin.'

Merrick, seated behind his desk again, studied his guest with more than a little interest. He reached out and took a couple of large cigars from the box on his desk. He clipped the ends of both and handed one to Blanchard, then struck a Lucifer and leaned over to light it. When they both had the cigars burning satisfactorily Merrick sat back and studied Blanchard.

'I think it's time we got to the real reason you're here, because it isn't just to make small talk about my home.'

Blanchard drew on his cigar, blowing blue smoke at the ceiling.

'We were expecting matters to have progressed further than they have, Yancey. A few of the investors have been expressing a little disquiet at the delays.' Blanchard spread his arms. 'Now I stand in your corner. You know that. But with the kind of money involved, not to mention the future potential of this project, some of our more nervous friends are starting to show their true colors. Just remember, Yancey, that there are influential men behind this venture. They get uncomfortable if things don't go their way.'

He watched for Merrick's reaction, his face impassive. Blanchard had a habit of stretching the moment, letting the other man sweat if need be. Merrick had realized this earlier in their relationship and understood the game. So he returned the favor, not allowing what he was thinking to show.

'Henry Conway is more than simply a small local rancher,' he said. 'The man has a spread that matches the Diamond-M. A large crew behind him. And he is a well-respected member of the community. I can't ride in and wipe him out with a single raid.'

'Easy questions, Yancey. Do you want to make money? Do you want the power this deal will bring?'

Merrick waved a hand around the room. 'Look at what I have here. Does it look like I'm a man who settles for second best?'

Blanchard gave that sly smile. He drained his tumbler and indicated he wanted more. Merrick obliged, filling the tumbler and passing it back.

'I was born into a comfortable life,' Merrick said. 'Nothing fancy but from the time I was old enough to understand I knew it wasn't enough. I moved on. Worked damned hard and took every opportunity I could. It paid off. That's why I'm where I am today.'

'But you want more,' Blanchard said. 'A lot more.'

'Damn right I do.'

'The line has to go through. All the way to Beecher's Crossing. And once we reach it there's no reason the tracks can't go further. Lots of land out there. The railroad will bring in even more business. Railroads are the lifeblood of a growing country, boy. They bring people. Business. And they bring success to the people who have the vision to build them. The Lazy-C stands in our path. Can't let that happen. Too much has already been invested. You have a foothold. Stay the course and you'll have a damn sight more.'

Merrick saw the vision through the haze of rising cigar smoke. His vision for the future of the basin, of which he was a part.

Blanchard said, 'Conway has already been affected. We need to hit him again. Before he can recover. We lose the chance now we might not get a second one.' He leaned forward, face tight. 'Money. Men. Anything you need. It's there for the asking. And if people standing in our way get hurt, well it's the price for getting what we want.'

12

They saw the fire well before reaching the ranch. The blaze lit up the night sky. Spurring their horses the Texans covered the last mile to the Lazy-C in quick time. As the came into the yard they could see that one of the big barns was well ablaze, sparks jumping out of the flame and smoke. Conway's on-hand crew were dousing the flames as best they could with buckets of water from the deep well in the yard.

Out of their saddles Ballard and McCall joined Henry and Helen Conway as they stood watching. Laney Chancery saw them and came across.

'They took Chris,' he said. 'Must have been watching and when she come out to feed her horse they rode in across the yard and grabbed her. Riders just came in out of the dark. Couple were shooting off guns like bullets were going out of fashion. Two others rode by the barn, dousing it with oil. One had a burning torch and he set the fire before they just went hell for leather.'

'We couldn't shoot back for fear of hitting Chris,' Conway said.

'Anybody hurt?' McCall asked.

'Jim Coolidge was hit in the leg,' Chancery said. 'He'll be okay. He's just mad he won't be able to ride when we go lookin' for Chris.'

'Recognize any of them?' Ballard said.

'Rafe Kershaw was riding with them,' Helen Conway said. 'I saw his face when they rode by the burning barn.'

'See which way they rode out?' McCall said.

'Cut off to the west,' Chancery said.

McCall nodded to that. 'Had a feeling you were going to say that.'

'It mean something?'

'It does.'

'Henry?' Ballard said.

'We have to get her back, Chet. We already lost our son. Can't allow it to happen to Chris.'

'That's what Merrick is counting on,' Ballard said. 'He'll be waiting for you to step away from the Lazy-C this time.'

Conway put an arm around his wife. Glanced at her strained expression. Any decision he made was going to tear him apart. He was going to lose whichever way he chose if things went bad.

'Can you get her back?' Helen asked, her gaze fixed on Ballard.

'You trust me?' he asked.

Helen smiled tiredly. 'You know the answer to that, Chet Ballard. Same goes for Jess.'

'Then you go talk to Merrick. Tell him whatever he wants to hear.'

'You mean lie to him?'

McCall smiled. 'All the way down to the toes of your boots, ma'am. Play his game and let him think he's won.'

'Go bring Chris back,' Helen said. 'We'll go to town and make Yancey Merrick a happy man — for as long as it takes for you to get back and knock the smile off his face.'

'You heard the boss,' Henry Conway said. 'Let's pray we can do this.'

As they made for the stable to get fresh horses Laney Chancery walked with them.

'Anything you boys need?'

'Extra ammunition. Couple filled canteens. Plenty of luck,' McCall said.

'First things I can do,' Chancery said. 'Can't do more than wish you the luck.'

'That'll have to do,' Ballard said.

They were saddling up when Ballard glanced at his partner.

'How close is this guess of yours?' he asked.

'Pretty thin as guesses go, but it's all we got.'

'You want to explain?'

'I don't figure Merrick is going to hold Chris in town. Not with Ray Bellingham around. He'll want to stay on the right side until he has Henry's name on a legal document.'

'Sounds sensible. So not Beecher's Crossing. Where else?'

'Laney said they rode out to the west.'

'Don't make me keep asking.'

'Chet, what's out there?'

'Not a lot. Empty country after you get by those deserted spreads. Jess, you don't think they have Chris locked up in one of the abandoned ranches?'

McCall shook his head. 'Not after they tried it with you at the Morrissey place. Now, I'm thinking they'll take her where they'll have plenty of backup. A bunch of guns around them.'

Ballard's expression changed the moment he saw what his partner was getting at.

'Son of a bitch,' he said. 'The railhead?'

13

By mid-morning Ballard and McCall were in position behind the construction site. They had ridden through the darkness, circling around the camp, well away from any possible watching eyes. At one point they had spent some time observing the place under cover of a scrub-topped ridge. Apart from a couple of casual guards, obviously bored by the routine of watching over sleeping men and cook fires, there was no movement. The guards seemed more inclined to keep topping up their coffee mugs and rolling fresh cigarettes than doing their job.

'Doesn't seem your visit left them feeling threatened,' Ballard said dryly.

'I guess I forgot to say boo and pull a fierce face. That might have made the difference.'

They stayed and watched the camp

for a little while longer, observing the layout as best they could in the darkness. When they moved on, leading their horses, they continued to circle the area until they were well behind the place. They chose a spot out of sight and tethered their horses in a deep thicket. In the time before dawn they made sure their rifles and handguns were fully loaded.

'We'll only get one chance at this,' Ballard said. 'There isn't going to be much time for reloading. So make your shots count.'

'I'm guessing the construction gang isn't going to be armed,' McCall said. 'As long as they stay out of it no need to get righteous with them. Just watch for that big feller, Bell. Boss man with the gun crew. Bad disposition to go with his size. Top man is Collhurst. Smooth-looking hombre with a fancy way of dressing. Makes out to be friendly, but I wouldn't turn my back on him.'

The locomotive, with the coupled

cars, was building up a head of steam as dawn broke. McCall noted that the rear car looked like a personal coach, most likely Bruce Collhurst's. It was painted in a fancy color scheme and gleamed under the thin layer of Texas dust.

'You thinking that might be where they have Chris?' Ballard said.

'I can see Collhurst playing the host,' McCall said. 'Putting on all the airs and graces for her. Being a gentleman.'

The way McCall spoke the word he made it sound downright crude.

'Hey, partner, look who just crawled out of his blanket,' Ballard said.

McCall followed the pointing finger and saw Rafe Kershaw emerging from one of the crew tents. From the way he was arching his back it didn't appear he'd had a comfortable night.

'Boss Collhurst didn't invite him to share the coach,' McCall said.

They watched Kershaw cross to Collhurst's rail car. The man himself appeared to stand on the small platform, talking to Kershaw. When

Collhurst retreated back inside the car Kershaw made his way across to the cook fires and helped himself to a mug of coffee. A familiar, massive figure showed and joined Kershaw.

Cleve Bell.

'That the one you were telling me about?' Ballard asked. 'I see what you were saying. That is one big hombre.'

While the construction crew and Bell's gunhands helped themselves to the food prepared by the cook and his helper, Ballard and McCall worked their way around the stacked building materials. The piles of steel rails, the heavy wooden ties. Wooden casks of iron spikes, construction tools. They took up a large area. It was easy for them to stay hidden behind the mass of goods. At the far end of the material stored was a wooden shed with a black painted sign on the door.

Danger. Explosives. No naked lights.

McCall studied the legend, a slow smile creasing his face.

'Nice way to start the day with a bang,' he said.

'Get their attention,' Ballard agreed.

They snapped back the bolt on the door and peered inside. The hut was packed with casks of explosive powder and cases of dynamite. McCall picked up a thick coil of fuse.

'While they have their chow we work,' he said.

They carried out a number of casks and moved around the stacked construction materials. Placing the casks they opened the lids and inserted lengths of fuse. Once this was done McCall placed a final cask just inside the door of the hut. They paused a number of times to check that the feeders were still eating and no one was paying any undue attention.

'Start with the furthest cask,' McCall said. 'Light the fuses and then we get the hell back into cover.'

They took out the Lucifers they carried to light their cigarettes, then separated to set the fuses. Ballard understood the principle of fuses having a burn time but he didn't feel entirely comfortable with the actual operation. Even so he did what was expected, then pulled back through the material stacks and was hard on McCall's heels when they exited the area. He didn't feel completely safe until they were both back behind the cover they had chosen earlier.

It seemed a long time for the fuses to burn down. McCall was beginning to wonder whether the idea was going to work and even though they were both anticipating the blasts the eruptions caught them unaware.

The first explosion shattered the morning stillness. It was far louder than McCall had expected. The ground shook. Though they couldn't see it, the blast threw earth and rocks into the air, along with steel rails. Other explosions followed in a chorus of noise. One after the other the planted casks of powder ripped the day apart. The steel rails were followed by splintered ties, the shredded timber flying in all directions. Iron spikes were turned into deadly missiles that were hurled around in a whistling shower.

The final explosion, as the powder store blew, was the largest of all. When the stored powder and dynamite blew the blast roared skywards in a huge ball of flame and accompanying smoke. The fireball rose to a surprising height, heat and the shock wave freezing everyone in the area as it spread out. Even Ballard and McCall, sheltered by the rocky ridge that hid them, were battered by the effect. The ground under them rippled like it was fluid and they were engulfed by the thick cloud of gritty dust that followed. The rumble of the explosions echoed around them as they fought to get to their feet and move in on the camp before Bell's men recovered their wits.

Debris was still dropping from the swirling dust as Ballard and McCall reached the camp. Men were scattering back and forth, yelling and calling to each other.

'I'll go and see if Chris is in that fancy car,' Ballard said. 'Go and get your hands on Kershaw.'

McCall nodded, turning in the opposite direction as he strode through the wrecked site. The last sighting he had of Kershaw was by the cook fire.

The Texan saw figures emerging from the dust cloud. A dust-caked man loomed up, blinking his streaming eyes. He was clutching a handgun, and the moment he saw McCall he raised the weapon and fired. The .45 slug burned past McCall. The Winchester in McCall's hands snapped out a shot and the shooter stumbled back, the slug in his chest.

Behind the falling man another shape emerged from the dispersing dust. McCall didn't need a second look at the hulking form. He knew instantly who it was.

Cleve Bell.

14

The man moved fast, reaching McCall before he could bring his rifle on target. A huge hand slapped the Winchester aside, sending it spinning out of McCall's grip. Bell's big hands caught hold of McCall and dragged him close, sliding up to clutch at his throat.

'Glad you could make it, bucko,' Bell said. 'I just knew you'd come back.'

McCall felt thick, powerful fingers clamp around his throat, cutting off his ability to breath. He dropped one hand to his holstered revolver, hauling it free, but Bell, anticipating the move, reached down with his left hand and crushed the Texan's fingers against the weapon, preventing him from using the Colt. The hand still gripping McCall's throat tightened. With the span of his single hand Bell was able to engulf McCall's throat easily.

Mrs McCall, your boy is in trouble, McCall thought.

The Colt dropped from numb fingers. McCall used both hands to pummel at Bell's thick body. Nothing seemed to have any effect and as Bell increased his grip McCall felt his strength fading. He was staring into Bell's face, seeing the caked dust. Blood sliding down the man's cheek from a gash. Bell's eyes were wide open, staring, wild with the rage that was burning behind them. He used his free hand to punch McCall and those blows were bruising McCall's ribs prior to breaking the bones.

McCall managed to land a telling blow over the bleeding cut in Bell's cheek. It tore the flesh further and blood welled from the wound. Bell flicked his head sideways like a man chasing off an irritating insect. McCall repeated the blow, spreading more blood across Bell's face. He knew his punches were weakening as the lack of oxygen affected him. McCall knew if he didn't do something drastic he was going to pass out.

Drastic, his brain was telling him. *Do something he isn't going to expect. The man is going to choke you. You have to . . .*

McCall held Bell's wild stare for a couple of seconds.

Then he raised both his hands, clamped them against the man's face, and jabbed his thumbs into Bell's eyes. He dug them in hard, working the extended digits in deep. He ignored the feel of warm fluid that burst free, closed his ears to Bell's agonised scream as pain rose. McCall felt the slippery mass of the eyeballs as they were forced from the sockets, the spurt of liquid streaming down Bell's face.

The hands around McCall's throat released their grip. He stumbled back, sucking air into his aching lungs, dropping to his knees as he reached for the gun he'd been forced to let go. Closing his hands around the Winchester McCall swung the rifle around as he saw one of Bell's gunmen moving toward him. He didn't hesitate. McCall triggered the rifle and saw the man fall back. A second gunhand stepped aside as the man went down. McCall worked the Winchester's lever and fired off a trio of shots that put this one down as well.

A harsh roar from Bell reached McCall's ears. The big man, blood running down his face from his eyes, was lurching forward blindly, his own revolver in his hand. He was waving the weapon back and forth and it fired without warning, the slug burning the air to one side. Bell cocked and fired again and McCall felt the slug clip his sleeve. He didn't hesitate, turning the Winchester and putting a shot into Bell's head, inches over his sightless eyes. Then a second.

'Son of a bitch,' McCall heard.

McCall recognized Rafe Kershaw's voice. The man was a few yards away, watching as Bell went down, snatching at his own handgun. It was only halfway out of the holster when McCall put a .44–40 slug in Kershaw's left leg, above the knee. Kershaw gasped, letting go his gun and clutching both hands to his thigh. Blood wet his pants leg, squirting through his fingers. Slumping to the ground Kershaw suddenly lost interest in what was going on around him.

The activity around McCall had slackened off as Bell's gunhands moved back, seeing Bell go down and realizing that their employment was fast fading. McCall understood the way their minds worked. They were paid to work for the railroad. Once the incentive was removed they were unemployed and being who they were they would see no profit fighting for a lost cause.

McCall watched as the remaining gunhands faded away, making for the picket line on the far side of the camp. He maintained his stance, the Winchester held ready if any of them suddenly had a change of heart. He didn't believe that would happen. They were already out of pocket and bullets cost money.

He touched his sore throat. That was going to hurt for a time and he'd have one hell of a bruise.

Behind him he heard a crash of sound coming from the rail car.

That, he figured, *would be Ballard*.

15

Ballard was in no mood for distractions. He used his rifle to clear a way to Collhurst's rail car, emptying the full magazine at the gunhands who briefly blocked his way. By the time he reached the ornate car there were no more gunhands and his Winchester was empty. Ballard let the rifle go and took out his Colt. He hauled himself up the steps and onto the platform at the back of the car. The door swung open and a lone figure filled the entrance, a shotgun held across his chest. Ballard didn't even pause for breath. He thrust the Colt forward and put two shots into the man, reaching out to pull him clear. The bodyguard, dead on his feet, crumpled to the platform, and Ballard stepped inside.

The first thing he saw was Chris Conway. Slumped in a padded seat she looked angry as a wet hen. Her clothes were creased, her hair mussed and she had a bruise across her right cheek. When she recognized Ballard's dust-caked form a weary smile crossed her face.

Bruce Collhurst, urbane and seemingly unruffled by the recent events, was leaning against the oak desk that filled the far end of the expensively furnished private car.

'Is this your knight in shining armor?' Collhurst said peevishly.

Ballard kept moving as he cleared the door, his long legs carrying him down the car. As he passed Chris he dropped his Colt in her lap.

'Hold this.'

He increased his pace as he closed in on Collhurst. The railman must have realised he was in trouble, raising a hand to ward off the Texan, but it was a useless gesture. Ballard slammed into him, the impact carrying them over the desk. They crashed to the floor on the far side, knocking the leather chair

146

aside. Ballard swung himself upright, hands gripping the front of Collhurst's shirt as he dragged the man to his feet. He drove a bunched fist into Collhurst's face. Blood spurted from crushed lips as the railman was sent reeling. Ballard stepped in close and delivered blow after blow, pushing the man across the car. Collhurst made an attempt to fight back but he was no match for the big Texan's fury. He drove Collhurst back and forth across the car, the man spilling blood down his front in a glistening stream. In the end he didn't even attempt to block Ballard's blows. It came to an end when Ballard took hold of Collhurst and swung him round, hurling him head first through the side window of the car.

As Collhurst disappeared in a shower of broken glass Ballard leaned against the desk, flexing his bloody fists, and glanced across at Chris.

'You been hurt in any way, Chris?'

The young woman managed a smile as she handed the Colt back to Ballard.

'Apart from the bruises, no, and especially not in the way you're concerned about.'

Ballard holstered the revolver. 'Good to hear, young lady.'

When they emerged from the car they were met by McCall.

'Before you ask, Jess, my virtue has not been sullied,' Chris said.

'More than can be said for Collhurst,' McCall said. 'Looks like he landed hard.'

The railman's head lay at an unnatural angle from where he had hit the hard ground.

'Will you take me away from here, please,' Chris said, turning away.

16

An hour before dusk the inhabitants of Beecher's Crossing were witness to the group of riders coming into town and reining in outside The Golden Lady: Ballard, McCall and Chris Conway, with a semiconscious Rafe Kershaw clinging to his saddle. Ray Bellingham, summoned from his office, met them along with Henry Conway and his wife. There was a brief reconciliation when the Conways recognized their daughter.

'What happened to you?' Helen Conway asked when she saw the state they were in.

'It got a little dusty,' Ballard said.

They hadn't been able to clean up since leaving the rail camp and the dust and grime was still clinging to them.

'Merrick still inside?' McCall asked.

'Feeling pretty pleased with himself,' Henry Conway said.

'He believes the paper we signed hands him the Lazy-C on a plate,' Helen said.

As they gathered on the boardwalk Ballard said, 'Time we put him right.'

'Let's go, Kershaw,' McCall said, hauling the wounded man upright.

'Jess?' Bellingham said.

'You think I'm going in there to shoot him?'

'Wouldn't surprise me.'

'Marshal,' Chris said, 'I want Yancey Merrick charged with kidnapping me. Kershaw here took me by force on Merrick's behalf.'

Bellingham rounded on Kershaw. 'That true?'

'Yeah.' He slumped down on the bench set against the wall outside the saloon, hugging his bloody leg.

Bellingham turned to his deputy. 'Get doc out here to look at his damn leg. And don't let him out of your sight.'

With Ballard and McCall in the lead they pushed through the door into the

150

saloon. It was relatively quiet inside, there were only a few customers. At the top end of the big room, at the table always reserved for Merrick, the man himself, accompanied by Orrin Blanchard, was bent over a sheaf of documents. When he became aware of their presence he sat back in his seat. The satisfied smirk on his face faded when he saw Chris Conway.

'Surprised to see me?' she said.

'Why should I be?' Merrick said.

'Seeing as how you sent your men to the Lazy-C to force me to go with them to the rail camp.'

'I have no idea what this woman is talking about,' Merrick said hurriedly.

'Don't say another word,' Blanchard said. 'My lawyers will deal with this.'

'Better make sure they have it all,' Bellingham said. 'Kidnapping. The attempted poisoning of Lazy-C water. The killing of Harry Conway.'

'None of it is true.'

'Not according to your man Kershaw,' Ballard said. 'He's been talking pretty convincingly on the ride in from the rail camp.'

'*Kershaw?* He . . . '

'He's outside right now and I'll be getting a written statement from him as soon as the doc's tended to him,' Bellingham said.

'Face it, Merrick. It's done,' McCall said. 'Your scheme has been blown sky high — literally. Surprising what a few barrels of black powder can do.'

'I'll have my lawyers onto you,' Blanchard threatened. 'If any damage has been done to the rail camp.'

'You can guarantee that,' Ballard said.

'We will reorganize. Bring in more people. Now we have the rights to cross Lazy-C land you can't stop us.'

'What rights?' McCall asked casually.

Merrick pushed at the paperwork on the table and gave a harsh laugh as he lifted a legal document, brandishing it at them.

'Here. All legal. Signed by Henry Conway a couple of hours ago.'

'That right?' McCall said. 'Legal and binding? Seems he's got you there, Henry. You want to show me that signature, Merrick?'

McCall reached out and took the document from Merrick's hand, studying it intently.

'Signed and dated,' Merrick said, ignoring the alarm that crossed Orrin Blanchard's face.

McCall nodded slowly as he examined the document.

'What do you figure, Marshal?'

'Looks that way to me,' Bellingham said.

'You sign this?' McCall asked Conway and Conway nodded. 'Easy as that. Just one piece of paper and it's done.'

Orrin Blanchard pushed up out of his seat, his face dark with suspicion.

'Give me that.'

McCall had pulled a match from his shirt pocket. He thumbed it alight and held it to one corner of the document.

'No!' Merrick screamed.

He couldn't reach across the table as

he saw the flame creeping across the paper.

Blanchard lunged forward, pushing Helen Conway aside as he made a grab for the document.

'Out of my way, you damned . . . '

Chet Ballard caught hold of Blanchard's shirt front and hauled him round, then swung his big right fist back. When he hit Blanchard the meaty sound could be heard across the saloon. Blanchard went backwards, bounced off the edge of the table and crashed to the floor.

'Excitable sort isn't he,' Helen Conway said.

Yancey Merrick, screaming with rage, pushed the table aside, reaching under his coat to drag out a stubby barrelled pistol as he made a futile grab for the burning document.

The sound of a shot made them all step back.

Merrick dropped his weapon and clutched at his right arm.

Stepping forward Ray Bellingham,

smoking pistol in his hand, yanked Merrick aside.

'Way things are going,' he said, 'we're going to need a bigger jail.'

Merrick stared at the burned document as McCall let it flutter to the saloon floor where he ground the black ashes to dust under his boot.

'So what document were we talking about?' he asked finally.

'Never seen any document,' Bellingham said. 'And you, Mister Blanchard, better be ready to climb on board the stage when it leaves in the morning.' He shook Merrick by the collar. 'All that talk of lawyers, Merrick. I suggest you get yourself a good one, 'cause by the time I work on the list of charges against you he's going to be earning every penny you'll need to pay him.'

17

They took rooms at Beecher's Crossing's best hotel. It was in fact the only hotel in town. Ballard and McCall made a visit to a store where they bought fresh clothes to replace the filthy outfits they were wearing. After baths and shaves, dressed in their new finery they all congregated in the dining room and had a meal.

Over a glass of wine Henry Conway had ordered they offered a toast to Harry Conway's memory.

'I would like to say thank you,' Helen said. 'To Chet and Jess for their help. We owe you both.'

'I'll second that.' Henry agreed.

'We couldn't do anything else,' McCall said. 'You pay our wages, boss man.'

'And don't forget what they did for me,' Chris said. 'I'll own up to being frightened by that man Collhurst.'

'Well he isn't going to . . . ' Ballard began to say.

At that moment the peaceful atmosphere was shattered by a couple of shots that came from beyond the hotel.

As Ballard and McCall came to their feet, making for the exit, more gunfire erupted. The pair went through the hotel lobby and out the door.

'That came from the jail,' Ballard said.

'Not wrong there, son,' McCall agreed.

He had snatched his Colt from its holster as he exited the dining room. The hotel rules decreed that all gunbelts be hung from the hooks provided on entering the dining room.

It was still light enough on the street — with additional illumination coming from the lamps lit — to see a lone figure on hands and knees crawling across the boardwalk outside the jail's open door. McCall recognized Ray Bellingham's deputy, Cyrus Makin. There was a discarded shotgun on the boardwalk a few feet from the deputy.

'A guess,' McCall said, 'but I figure we've had a breakout.'

He moved in the direction of the jail as he saw movement at the wide open door.

Ballard was annoyed with himself for not grabbing his own gun. He turned as a figure appeared at his side. It was Chris Conway. The young woman raised a hand, showing what she was holding.

'You forgot something,' she said.

'Obliged,' Ballard said. 'Now you step back inside.'

He took off after his partner who had already covered half the distance to the jail.

'Behind you, Jess,' he called.

There was more movement in the light of the jail door. Someone called out. An angry voice. A gun crashed and a figure spun out over the boardwalk and onto the street.

Ray Bellingham.

'Ain't keepin' me in your damn jail,' a man screamed defiantly.

A figure silhouetted in the light blocked the jail door, a gun in his hand. He fired at Bellingham, a gout of flame shooting from the muzzle. The Marshal was half turned by the force of the striking slug and started to fall. A second shot drove at his slumping figure.

'Sonofabitch,' McCall shouted, still moving forward.

The shooter was joined by a second man and they burst out of the jail door, parting as they came onto the board-walk. In the spill of light McCall was able to recognize Rafe Kershaw, lean face taut with anger, and close by him Yancey Merrick. They were both armed with rifles, with handguns pushed behind their belts.

'Give it up,' McCall called as he barrelled along the street. 'Nowhere to go.'

'That so,' Kershaw called back. 'We'll see . . .'

He brought up his rifle and levered off a trio of shots that punched into the dirt around McCall — who kept coming — his big Colt steady in his hand. It was almost as if time took a pause as McCall threw out his arm, drew back the hammer and triggered a shot that hammered home in Kershaw's chest. The impact brought Kershaw up short, his face expressing shock. McCall came to a stop, fisting his pistol in both hands and put two more .45 slugs into Kershaw. The man went down on the boardwalk, his body rolling over onto the street.

Ballard had moved up behind his partner, taking a step to one side as he saw Yancey Merrick levelling his own rifle at McCall. The Texan brought his pistol into play, hammer clicking back even as it centered on Merrick. The shot punched in through the side of Merrick's head, coring through and blowing out in a burst of bloody debris. Merrick stiffened briefly, then toppled back and slid down the wall of the jail to curl up against the boardwalk.

In the following silence came a soft groan. It came from Cyrus Makin.

When McCall bent over him he saw the bloody wound in the deputy's left shoulder. The slug had burned its way from back to front, leaving behind a mushy hole.

'My fault,' Makin whispered, face wet with sweat. 'I turned my back for couple of seconds when I went to pick up Kershaw's empty plate. Never expected him to move so fast, what with him having that wounded leg . . . '

'We called for the doctor,' Chris Conway said from behind McCall.

Helen Conway appeared. She bent over Makin. 'You set easy there, Cyrus.'

'. . . my fault,' he was mumbling. 'My fault.'

'You hush now. Nobody's fault but those two.'

'How's Ray?' Henry Conway asked.

Ballard was kneeling beside the lawman, checking him over.

'Be close, but I think he'll come through.'

Bellingham stirred. Looked up at Ballard.

'How's Cyrus?'

'Blaming himself for it all.'

'Oh hell,' Bellingham said, 'that boy allus was a worrier.' He reached out a hand to grasp Ballard's arm. 'Kershaw. Merrick. You get her done?'

'All the way,' Ballard told him. 'Sorry about the mess on your boardwalk.'

They heard the doctor coming and Ballard told Bellingham to rest easy. He pushed to his feet and crossed to where McCall was quietly standing clear of the growing crowd.

'Son, how come we got half the town here now the fuss has died down? Where were they a few minutes ago?'

'Got me there, partner.'

'Be glad to get back to the Lazy-C,' McCall observed. 'In general moving a herd of cows around tends to be a whole lot more peaceable.'

Ballard had to agree to that.

'So let's get back to home,' he said. And they did . . .

BALLARD & McCALL:
TWO FROM TEXAS

We do hope that you have enjoyed reading this large print book.

Did you know that all of our titles are available for purchase?

We publish a wide range of high quality large print books including:
Romances, Mysteries, Classics
General Fiction
Non Fiction and Westerns

Special interest titles available in large print are:
The Little Oxford Dictionary
Music Book, Song Book
Hymn Book, Service Book

Also available from us courtesy of Oxford University Press:
Young Readers' Dictionary
(large print edition)
Young Readers' Thesaurus
(large print edition)

For further information or a free brochure, please contact us at:
Ulverscroft Large Print Books Ltd.,
The Green, Bradgate Road, Anstey,
Leicester, LE7 7FU, England.
Tel: (00 44) **0116 236 4325**
Fax: (00 44) **0116 234 0205**

REAPER

Lee Clinton

The Indian Territory is a hellhole of lawlessness. Deputies are gunned down in cold blood, and outlaws are trading arms to renegades. In desperation, a bold and secret plan is designed by two senior US marshals — recruit a new and unknown deputy, who can operate independently to hunt down and kill three notorious outlaws in reprisal. But has the right man been selected? Walter Garfield's background seems more than a little shady, and he appears to have his own agenda . . .

TEXAS VENGEANCE

Ralph Hayes

Luther Bastian's younger brother was murdered by outlaws. Now Bastian is a bounty hunter who comes to kill — unable to be reasoned with, persuaded or bribed. So when a gang of lawless men brutally slay a Texas Ranger, Captain Mallory knows just the man to call on. But during the pursuit, Bastian is befriended by a young woman and a small boy. Can they change his view on the world, and put an end to his quest for vengeance?

SADDLER'S RUN

Harriet Cade

Ben Saddler, sometime soldier of the Confederate Army, has had many jobs: scout, gambler, barkeep, deputy sheriff, road agent, cowboy . . . Now he is a whiskey runner trying to scrape a living in the Indian Territories. His life takes an unexpected turn when he suddenly finds himself responsible for a young girl. Somehow, he must escort her to safety; evade capture by the law; outgun those who would kill him; and negotiate his way through an Indian uprising. Can he succeed?

LONG SHADOWS

Clyde Barker

For many years, Colonel Robert Farrance has lived a respectable life. Nobody knows that his present prosperity is founded upon his earlier life as a ruthless and determined bandit. Then a figure from his past arrives in town, threatening to expose his history — and asking Farrance to assist him in securing his lost proceeds from a long-ago train robbery. The colonel acquiesces. But triumph looks to turn to tragedy when Farrance stands to lose all that he holds most precious . . .

MEDICINE FEATHER

Will DuRey

Prospectors in the hills are being ambushed and killed by a gang determined to snatch every ounce of gold that is dug from the ground or panned from the streams. But when one such attack earns the robbers nothing but a pack of pelts, it sets in motion a chain of events leading to a bloody conclusion. For the victim — Medicine Feather, brother of the Arapaho and friend of the Sioux — is unwilling to relinquish his possessions without seeking revenge . . .